Some men of seventy-two might be content to sit home with their memoirs, their sherry, and their dogs, but General Ransom Jarvis was not one of them. He was profoundly bored. Worse, he was broke, and his housekeeper would not lend him any money. Even worse, his son was running for governor and would expect the General to stay out of trouble until the campaign was over.

It was enough to drive a man to wild and reckless deeds—and it did.

"The book . . . emerges tender, very funny, and beautifully worked out."
San Francisco Chronicle

"An intelligent, well-written thriller."
London Daily Mirror

DEATH OF AN OLD SINNER

Dorothy Salisbury Davis

BALLANTINE BOOKS • NEW YORK

Originally published in hardcover by Charles Scribner's Sons in 1957.

Library of Congress Catalog Card Number: 57-6064

ISBN 0-345-34662-9

Manufactured in the United States of America

First Ballantine Books Edition: October 1987

1

On gray days General Jarvis was restless. He loathed the country, he loathed the house, a rambling, rattling affair in the wind which seemed now when he was approaching old age, to be making the same ghostly insinuations with which it had mocked him in his childhood. In those days it had boasted its Hudson River lore, a hideaway for river pirates, a refuge for runaway slaves, its acquaintance with men like Major André and Benedict Arnold, Rip Van Winkle, Ichabod Crane, the first Dutch burghers . . . Lies all, of course, to be perpetrated only in a child's mind. The house was Victorian. But now, he thought, looking down to the drifts of snow which sloped to the drop above the river's edge, it told an obvious truth: for all its groans and sighs, it would survive him by at least a generation.

"Oh, do be quiet," he said, returning to his desk. That, too, was a nasty habit of age—old people forever talking to inanimate things: abusing a rocker, begging the fire not to go out on them. He looked at the title on the folder before him: *The Memoirs of Major General Ransom Jarvis, U.S. Army, Retired*.

Start it off with a few boyhood reminiscences, he had been advised. Well, he could remember fox hunting in Rockland County, and ice-boat racing on the Hudson above Hook Mountain. He remembered the coaches that met trains at the Piermont terminal a few miles south. He had held the horses while they loaded. And your ancestors, something about them. There was a president in the family, wasn't there? Not much of a president, the General thought now, looking up at the portrait of a face with an expression quite as sour as his own mood. And your military career, of course. Five continents, three wars. The General puffed his cheeks and exploded a blast of air that would have shivered

1

Ulysses. Some men at seventy-two might be content with their memoirs, their sherry, their dogs. His bored him to despair. The only things worth telling raised the question of libel, violation of other peoples' privacy, or some such nonsense, and might also vicariously injure the career of his promising son. Don't you mean the promising career of your son, General? he asked himself on behalf of some editorial inquisitor.

"No, by God! I mean my promising son. The things that lad has promised me . . ." The General rooted in the top drawer for his bank book, knowing exactly how little was tallied there and how long it needed to last him. He had already spent the advance payment on his memoirs, and thus far had made no more than a few skirmishes into its writing, neat little phrases in an elegant, old-fashioned law clerk's hand. That, indeed, was where he had learned to write, at the desk of his father's clerk. It was too bad, the General thought, snapping closed the bank book, that he hadn't been apprenticed to a forger in his youth. He might now be able to write a check someone in Nyack would honor; no one would honor one with his signature certainly.

He heard a door bang downstairs, and presently from the courtyard the off-key voice of Mrs. Norris as she raised it as high as the wind. She had been keeping the Nyack house for him since Jimmie was an infant and himself a widower, and she couldn't carry a better tune now than she could . . . how long? . . . oh my God, over forty years ago. It was unworthy of him, the General knew, but he could not avoid the thought of how her bank book must compare with his.

He decided to shave before going to her.

Mrs. Norris could have predicted, almost to the hour, the General's descent from his study. It was a great waste on the part of the United States Army to retire a man like him so early, but that, if there was any one thing she had learned of America in her forty-two years of residence, was typical of the whole country. Waste, waste, waste. A dire reckoning lay before it. She gave a great sigh at that thought; on the whole she would as soon it didn't come in her time. But she was convinced that the Lord kept a strict account book, all the same.

She had come over from Scotland at twenty, Mrs. Norris had, already a childless widow, and the truth was that over the years, adding a bit now and then to her husband's stature from what she took off that of other men, she probably loved him better now than ever she did in their brief marriage. He had been off to his last sailing within a week of their wedding. And she, having come out soon thereafter to her sister in Brooklyn, had almost as soon been eager for her independence. Starting as nurse for General Jarvis' son James, she had approved the house from the moment she put her foot inside the door, although to this day she did not altogether approve the General.

The old Mrs. Jarvis, the General's mother, had been alive then, and first laying eyes on Mrs. Norris, she had said of her within her hearing: "My dear, she looks just like the young Queen Victoria!" The resemblance had increased with the years and with the few odd pounds Mrs. Norris had put on here and there to where now she was a bit dumpy. When she went out, dressed in black with her head done up in a hat that would have nested a raven, it would have seemed a little more natural had she got into a carriage than an automobile.

The General was holding the door open for her when Mrs. Norris came in from the clothesline with the last of the sheets. Her nose was as red as pimento.

"Couldn't we strike a match, Mrs. Norris?" he said, with a nod at the open hearth, and a wink at his double meaning.

So, she thought, that's the mood he's in. He'll want to go into New York now, and she calculated the day of the month, and by it, the state of his finances. "Not for me," she said, "but if you're staying in my kitchen, light it."

"Not with that sort of invitation," he said, offended. He watched her folding sheets that had been unfolded to hang on the line. "Why in the name of God do you hang out clothes you've had finished?"

"They were laundry done, sir. I cannot abide the smell of public soap."

"Oh," said the General. "Have you ever smelt the public without soap?"

"I have," Mrs. Norris said.

And there didn't seem to be much future to that tack in the conversation. "During the war there were things you could buy on the other side with soap that you couldn't buy with money."

"What things?" Mrs. Norris snapped with the air of one tightening her hold on her convictions.

This was the day he was not going to get round her flank, the General realized, so he might as well make a direct assault. "You wouldn't have a few dollars about the house you could spare till the first, would you?"

"I would not. Mr. James said I could not give you any money while he was gone, sir."

The General clattered his heels on the brick floor. "I would remind you, Mrs. Norris, that Mr. James wasn't as big as a wink when you were hired."

"Yes, sir."

She was humble enough, he thought, when she had her money well buried. "Mr. James is now trying to hasten me into my dotage."

"If you hadn't put a lien on your pension, sir . . ."

"I should not have had an automobile! Or do you agree with Mr. James about that also, Mrs. Norris, that at my age I don't need an automobile?"

"I don't think you need a Jaguar, sir, if you want the truth."

"I don't want the truth!" the General roared. "What's so damned necessary about the truth all the time?"

Mrs. Norris drew her dumpy shape to its best height. "Oh, I'll say again what I've said many's the time in this house, if it wasn't for little Master Jamie, I'd give my notice."

"And many's the time if it wasn't for little Master Jamie, I'd have taken it. Little Master Jamie is forty-two years old!"

The General marched out of the kitchen and clacked his heels on the polished floor all the way back to his study. It was a terrible thing for a man to escape the discipline of military life into the tyranny of his family. Old generals, by God, should not be left to fade away. Like horses, they should be shot on becoming obsolete.

He shoveled the papers strewing his desk into the folder and gazed up at the portrait of his ancestor, the family's man of distinction—more or less. He had been a one term president of the United States. Unmarried, he had founded neither line nor fortune, unless, as Mrs. Norris would have said, it was done without his ken.

An unlikely situation that, by the looks of him. But bloody unfair it was to hang on the best wall in the house for a hundred or so years, and to have made no more contribution to the family than a clutter of papers in the attic and the reputation for having been one of the best forgotten presidents of your country.

Still, the General thought, knocking his pipe out in the fireplace, it was ungenerous to judge a man's looks by the fashion of his age in cravats; it would be very difficult for any face to rise above a thing like that looking less like an oyster than did granduncle. Nonetheless, you had to appraise him as his own times did—and his best recommendation for high office was his absence from the country in months of crisis. But then, so came generals also into politics oft-times, to the latterday destruction of their hard-won fame.

The General rested his backside on his desk and sucked on the empty pipe, gazing still at the portrait. "Not a memoir, not a biography," he said aloud. "Look at you— sitting there like a handpainted burp, an apt subject for neither gossip nor historian, your back to the wall, not a decade between you and oblivion. You know, Mr. President, you would have done much better by us to have kicked up your heels a bit, and I dare say, by yourself as well. A bit of scandal has saved many a nincompoop."

The General stuffed the bowl of his pipe and lit it. He went back to the desk chair then and from that vantage further studied the portrait. Get rid of that wrinkled sock around his neck and the old boy wouldn't look so fatuous. And it was the heavy eyelids that kept you from getting a good deep look into the man. No one was going to surprise his thoughts out of him. Really, the artist was a hack and the old boy likely knew it. He had sat for him as he had, no doubt, for Congressional bores and diplomatic con men—

because he had been told it was one of the things he needed to do to be president. He had put on a look he thought bespoke the cares of his office, and he came out like an old monk cowling the naughty thoughts in his eyes while he piously trolled the beads through his fingers.

"Tell me, Mr. President," the General said aloud again, "was there nothing in your life that could, shall we say, prosper us now? I have an open mind and an empty purse. Tell me the truth, is it worth my while to go up to the attic? To sort out that trunkful of papers? Eh, Mr. President?"

2

The sky was gray over Albany also at that hour, more snow starting to fall, great flakes of it clinging to the dirty hotel windows for an instant, slithering down then, down, down, down into vanishing rivulets. Jimmie Jarvis watched them, listening the while to the unending objections and justifications of himself in the blunt terms of political caucus.

Suddenly the men circling the table leaned back. Some lighted fresh cigars, some relighted stale ones. One of the two women present offered the other a king-sized cigarette. They all looked at Jimmie then, and their faces, friends' as well as foes', wore that slightly cynical expression which said in effect: all right, you're it. Why? Why you and not me?

Jimmie Jarvis—James Ransom Jarvis—rose, and fastened the middle button of his coat. That was a mistake, buttoning his coat. He could feel his heartbeat outside as well as within him. But he was not in the habit of correcting his mistakes in public. He put his hands in his trouser pockets and rocked back on his heels.

"My friends—and if you are not completely friendly, I direct myself even more to you—I am aware of the responsibility you will be offering me as well as the honor and the privilege—if you sustain until convention day the sentiment just expressed . . ."

Jimmie smiled then, seeing one after another of the delegates relax. He had put in enough "ifs" to assure them of his humility. He was forty-two, a bachelor, and seemed boyishly earnest in everything he did. And he had done many things in an already long public career. Ironically, his potential enemies here opposed him for the same reason his friends proposed him: he had once been New York District Attorney. There were men present who felt that a prosecutor was a dangerous man in any office, especially that of governor to which Jimmie now aspired. He looked from face to face of the men whose consent was still grudging. "You must remember, gentlemen, that as well as my hitch in the office of district attorney, I have also served in the United States House of Representatives. That I submit, would take the spurs off any cock."

This brought a crack in the great stone faces. At the moment there was no laughter in them.

"I have no speech to make, my friends, but I will answer frankly all questions."

Al Rogers rolled the cigar from the center of his mouth to the side of it. "Jimmie, wasn't your great-grand-uncle ambassador to somewhere before he was president of the country?"

Al had the subtlety of a tabloid newspaper: he was calling attention to the fact that there had been a president in Jimmie's family.

Jimmie nodded. "To the Court of St. James, I believe."

"We'd better hold it in confidence then," said an old timer with a trace of a brogue. "Unless you don't need to carry New York City."

"It'll be distinction enough," said Al, "that he's the great-grand-nephew of a president."

Jimmie winced at the endless commercial.

"Great-grand-nephew," another delegate weighed the words ponderously. "Wouldn't it be all right at this distance to call him your great-grandfather?"

"It might be risky, sir," said Jimmie, "his having been a bachelor."

And no one found that amusing. Jimmie sighed. It was fortunate that the people had more wit than their delegates, and maybe more wisdom.

But the subject of bachelorhood had been turned up again, as though it had not already been well explored: he had been cautioned to marry a widow before summer; no, better a young girl of modest means and no renown; but the best advice was finally calculated to be that of the two female delegates who were unanimous in their recommendation that he go before the people uncommitted in that regard; not a woman in the state then but would vote herself into the governor's mansion pulling the lever in his behalf.

With the bulldog air of having held onto one thought until he could spring it, Mike Zabriski waited till the lady's last remark and then said: "I don't suppose you've ever done anything in your life, young fella, that couldn't stand the scrutiny of the public eye?"

"I think, sir, the public eye would have long since found it," Jimmie said. "Look how it finds my father, every tumble he takes."

"An old man's tumbles, as you call them, are news—a young man's are maybe gossip. But in a man your age, they're dangerous."

In a man my age they are inevitable, Jimmie thought, but he put on a long face and said: "Yes, sir."

"Now answer my question," said Bulldog Mike.

Jimmie drew a deep breath. "I have been as honest as any man, Mike, and more discreet than most." To tell a lie as though it were the truth, he thought. But it was not a lie the way he had said it. Once only he had been less than cautious, and at a time in the world's history when caution was labeled the worth of fool's gold. And even in that instant, the cloak fate put about him and the lady resembled honor: she belonged to that noble race of people, who, if they were not proud of their sins, at least did not stoop to call them folly.

"That's good enough for me," said Mike, referring to Jimmie's avowal of honor and discretion.

With old Mike satisfied, no other delegate present dared complain. The meeting adjourned in good spirits. His enemies would not bare their fangs until he showed some weakness, and that was not to be at this, the king-making caucus. The Buffalo and New York timetables were already passing from hand to hand. Jimmie was bade by several gentlemen to give his father, the General, their warmest regards. He was asked if the old man would take to the stump on his behalf when the time came, and it was said that many an aging heart would flutter if the old boy strode out again.

Jimmie held Judge Turner's coat for him. He shrugged himself into it like a tired bear. The Judge, actually retired from the Appeals bench and a friend of his father's, would take upon himself more than ordinary arrangements in the forthcoming elections. He would try to arrange as well Jimmie's life for him. The Judge belonged to the Morals Squad of his party. He took Jimmie's arm. "It would be a fine thing to see your father in the reviewing stand for the St. Patrick's Day parade, a general in all his decorations."

"Better certainly than a mere major," said Jimmie, referring to his own rank in World War II.

"Is that as far as you got?" said the Judge as though a major were a very minor thing indeed.

Jimmie nodded.

"Didn't you go overseas?"

"Oh, yes. That I managed."

"Where?"

"I was stationed outside London," Jimmie said, wishing the Judge would get off the subject.

"Oh yes, yes. I remember. Well, just let your father stand in for you in matters military," he counseled. "I'll arrange it." Then as an afterthought: "How is he with the bottle these days?"

"Moderate," Jimmie said.

"And with the automobile?"

"More cautious than he used to be."

The Judge leaned closer to Jimmie after a glimpse around. One of the lady delegates stood nearby, her back to them. "And with the ladies?"

"More cautious than he used to be."

The Judge chuckled, forgetting then the temperate tune

he sang himself these days. "I remember him on our first leave after the Battle of the Marne. We were in France together, you know." He pulled himself up to a creaking attention. "Oh, by God, he was a man!"

As soon as Judge Turner marched off, Madeline Barker swung around and laid her fingers on Jimmie's arm. She had been a woman of great beauty, Jimmie thought. Much of it was there still as she ran on for fifty, but it was shadowed with bitterness, and more deeply now for her smile.

"I was outside London, too, during the war, Mr. Jarvis. I wonder it we do not have some friends in common."

Jimmie could feel a prickle at the back of his neck: a legitimate danger signal or merely his own conscience? It was a difficult distinction. "No doubt we call all Englishmen our friends," he said smiling and taking her hand. "Who could fail to, having lived with them?"

"And English women?" said Miss Barker.

Surely she was not that gauche! "What they lack in beauty, they atone in fervor," he said, tacking into the weather to test it for storm.

"And what they lack in fervor they atone in discretion," she said.

"I admire that quality in all people," Jimmie said with all the considerable suavity he could muster. He pressed her fingers slightly before releasing them. "I expect I shall lean a great deal on your support, Madeline."

She gave his fingers a little squeeze in return. "I am but a fragile Barker on the sea of politics," she said.

There was something ludicrous in the bad pun as well as in the notion of her fragility. Miss Barker had run twice for Congress, unsuccessfully. She was all but resigned now to the making and breaking of other candidates, sitting on the State policy committee, and apparently she was not above a bit of intimidation after the candidate was made.

"Forgive me for running off," Jimmie said, "but I want very much to catch this train. Call me in New York? I promise an excellent lunch?" He put it all like a question which she must answer for him. If necessary, he could have caught a later train, but he felt it imperative to put Miss Barker congenially in her place. To stay and court her company, even to buy her a drink would, he thought, show alarm at her suggestion of intimacy with his affairs.

"Thank you, Mr. Jarvis."

"Jimmie?" he prompted.

"Jimmie," she repeated, "good luck!"

It was said with such conviction, he once more doubted everything save his conscience. As he got into his coat, he wondered if he was as much a hypocrite as he felt at that moment. The possibility depressed him.

3

It was three days before Jimmie got home to Nyack, what with several things in a personal and business way to be put in quick order before the rumor of his candidacy got too far ahead of him. He talked to Mrs. Norris on the telephone, however, and confided that he was bringing home some rather extraordinary news.

Consequently the house was aglow with lights when he turned into the driveway, and as soon as he put his foot on the step, he could see the housekeeper bounce across the living room like a robin, pushing her bosom ahead of her. If this was not what some men would call home, Jimmie mused, many a man would settle for it as a better than fair substitute.

"Was it a provident trip, Mr. James?" the housekeeper inquired, taking his coat.

"In a way you might say it was, Mrs. Norris. And in another way, you might say it was expensive. Where's the old fellow?"

She threw up her hands. "He's been flying round like a bat in the attic for days. One minute he's sour as a quince, and the next he's skipping with glee. I'm very glad you're home, sir."

"Call him down," said Jimmie, "and I'll tell you the news . . . but in the strictest of confidence."

"I'm not in the habit of spouting, Mr. James. I leave that to your father."

"And bring some ice when you come," said Jimmie.

Just how the General would take the news, Jimmie didn't know. There was no doubt about it, the old boy liked things happening, and while he liked fame in the family, he preferred it to be his own. Now that he was retired he was touchier than ever about Jimmie's success. And sure enough, after making a few congratulatory remarks, he said, "I suppose having me for your father was something of a handicap?"

"Judge Turner helped me overcome that," Jimmie said.

"Did he?" the General snapped. "I thought I was making a joke."

"So did I, father. Actually, Judge Turner suggests that you might be willing to help me."

"In what way, may I ask?"

To tell him anything specific when he was in this mood, Jimmie thought was to get "no" for an answer. "Oh, a few personal appearances."

"At the old peoples' homes, I suppose."

Jimmie merely sighed.

So did Mrs. Norris, who, invited to have a drink on the occasion, sat now with her empty glass cupped in her hands like a votive offering. "Think of it: Master Jamie the Honorable James Jarvis, Governor of the Sovereign State . . ."

Jimmie shuddered as though she were casting a charm on him. "Have another drink, Mrs. Norris."

"The Honorable James Ransom Jarvis," the General corrected. "I suppose the campaign will cost a great deal of money?"

But of course, Jimmie thought, that was the burr now rubbing the old man. "I expect the party will make available enough money."

"Will it?" said the General, on the verge of sudden good humor.

"When the time comes I expect so. Are you broke, father?"

"Smashed."

"Well, that makes a pair of us. I've drawn all I can from the firm for the present." Jimmie turned to Mrs. Norris. "I suppose we'd better have dinner soon."

"Within the hour," she said, getting up. She gave Jimmie a great wink, always the mark of the "wee sup" in her. "And don't you worry about a thing, Mr. James."

The old man stomped out of the room ahead of her. "I'll be in my study when you're ready," he said.

"It's not as bad as I made it sound, Mrs. Norris," Jimmie confided when the General was gone. "But I can't have him making a touch this early in the month. What do you suppose he does with his money?"

"Fancy cars . . . and things," she said with Presbyterian ferocity.

Jimmie poured himself another drink, a long one, and took it up to his room. There he showered and changed into slacks and a wool shirt. Without a doubt, the old fellow needed something to occupy him, or better, a trip around the world. No, that was worse. He was quite capable of kicking up an international incident, of embarrassing the State Department as well as an ambitious son. There was a considerable file somewhere in the Pentagon on a roaring contest between Major General Jarvis and his Russian counterpart—the Russian drinking martinis, the General vodka. "You might say we got him home by an underground air-lift," a State Department wag had put it. Oh yes, quite capable of mischief was the General, and the hell of it was, the older he got, the greater his capabilities.

4

The General was sure he smelt the reek of conspiracy as he left the room ahead of Mrs. Norris. Caution. Every move weighted with caution. There was no gamble in the younger generation—all of them huddled behind the inevitability of the atom. Nothing to be ventured, no frontiers, no enterprise. Only caution. No wonder the boy had still, by report, the bulk of his inheritance from his mother.

The General slammed the door of his study and looked up at his unsung relative. "Catch hold of a star, old boy! You and I are going for a spin."

He kicked up the fire; then, taking an ashtray and his pen knife, he scraped some carbon from a burnt log. This he diluted with a drop of water, added a drop of iodine and finally some black ink. It would not do for the finished product—if there was going to be a finished product—but for the first experiment, it might do very well.

He had brought from the attic a fine red leather notebook, a diary, the binding scarcely faded by time. Inside, the excellent paper was yellowed ever so slightly, and the ink was fading through the years to a lighter brown. The diary he was by no means ready to touch—if ever he was going to touch it. He opened it to a half-empty page: the temptation was delicious. He put it by for the moment, locking the diary in the bottom drawer of his desk. He put the key beneath the frame of the President's picture.

He locked himself in his study then and took from a folder an old letter of his ancestor's; it had been written from England in his own hand, the subject a routine matter of diplomacy. The General, with military precision, took a nibbed pen in hand, dipped it into the concoction in the ashtray, exercised his arm on the desk, a circular motion, and added a postscript to the letter. "And Sylvia sends deep

14

love," he wrote, adding a replica of the President's signature. He counted to five and blotted it, securing thereby a paleness to his taste. The ink, he thought, surveying the whole, was almost as good an imitation as his handwriting. Ah, but that was imcomparable! Not for nought now, had he been stood long hours at the law clerk's desk as a boy, and made to imitate the briefs of the family firm, even as in his day, his father before him, and his grandfather, and likely, even granduncle. That he had deserted the law for the military was directly attributable to the distaste his clerking days gave him for the law.

He washed out the ashtray in the sink and then dabbed his finger with a bit of iodine to account for the smell of it, although in truth the smell was much like that of the diary itself. Well, he must look up the formula for ink in those days . . . if he was to need the ink. He had but turned the key in his door and sat down again at his desk when Jimmie knocked.

"Come in, come in, lad," he said, as though the key were never turned against a soul.

Jimmie looked down at the folder of old papers. "Don't tell me somebody's interested in them?"

"Oh, I'm sure the Library of Congress would house them if they were offered."

"I suppose we should do that," Jimmie said. "After all, they are state papers."

"For the most part they're rubbish, like all state papers," the old man said. "But look at this." Without a tremble of his hand, though his heart gave a sudden pounce, he pointed to the line he had forged a few minutes before.

Jimmie read it and lifted his eyebrows. "Who was Sylvia?"

"My very question," the old man said. "I've been three days searching for her in that trunk up there. Read that again."

Jimmie read it aloud this time: "And Sylvia sends deep love." He picked up the letter then and read it through. He gave it back. "Think you'll find her, father?"

His son's absolute and doubtless assumption of the letter's having been written, postscript and all, a hundred years before, tickled the old man almost to ecstasy. He needed now to guard himself carefully. "If I find her, Jimmie, it might make a different man of our—forebear."

"I don't think a change could hurt him, do you, father?"

"I do not. Nor do I think it would hurt you, his coming into the news again."

"Take it easy on that, father."

"I shall but tell the truth as I find it," the old man said piously.

"I think it's a fine undertaking, father. Really, in view of the work to be done on your own memoirs, this is very generous of you."

"I hope to be paid for it if they're published, you know. This is not altogether altruism."

Jimmie grinned. As though he had not known this to be back of the old boy's housekeeping. "Every cent he earns is yours, father. By the way, was Judge Turner in touch with you in the last day or so?" This was the question he had not dared ask downstairs.

"Uh-huh." The old man put away the folder.

"Well?" said Jimmie.

"Something about the Irish parade on St. Patrick's Day. I think he wanted me in the stands. I'm too busy now for that nonsense."

Well, Jimmie thought, going to the door without a word, if he was not going to help him, at least, involved in the family papers, neither would he hurt him. "As you like, father, as you like."

The old man cocked his head round at him. "Are you disappointed?"

"Of course, I'm disappointed! I'm about to run for governor of the state. My name is Jarvis. I'd like a hundred thousand or so Irishmen to remember it because General Jarvis saluted when they went marching by!"

"A hundred thousand or so, and every last holler of them with a flag in his hand! It'll be worse than the queen's coronation."

"All right, father. Thanks just the same."

The old man snapped his fingers and then held out his hand, without turning round or rising from his desk. "I'll need some money to get my decorations."

"Where are they?"

"Eighth Avenue somewhere, I think. I have the ticket."

"Oh, my God," said Jimmie, "they're in hock!"

The General swung around. "You would be surprised, my boy, at what good company that puts me in."

5

The next day, it being her afternoon off, Mrs. Norris rode into New York with the General. For all her deprecations of the Jaguar, she was quick enough to leap into it, he thought. She swathed her head—hat and all—in a scarf, locked her hands like a safety belt across her stomach, and gave a nod of her head for him to drive on.

"I suppose you're on your way to Brooklyn?" he said.

"I am, to my sister's," Mrs. Norris said. "You can drop me at the subway."

The General nodded. "How are the Robinsons?"

"Well enough for getting on. They always ask after you, sir."

"Do they?" said the General, and he wondered just what Mrs. Norris would say if she knew that he too would be seeing at least one of the Robinsons later in the day. Little she knew what a friendship had started on her introduction of Robbie and him the summer before. Robbie was an expert on horses, and therefore had a fair acquaintance with where and when the best of them were running. And that was but one of the Scotsman's useful hobbies, although it was the only one to date of which the General had taken advantage. "He's a printer, is he not?" the old man said for the sheer pleasure of deceiving her.

"Aye, and with his own shop and journeymen under him. Prospered he has with hard work. He came over an immigrant, too."

The General squinted round at her. "You look the soul of prosperity, Mrs. Norris."

She loosed one hand from the other long enough to show the fingers of the glove. "Darned and stitched, sir, but respectable."

"As a lily," said the General, disgusted with the alarm she took if there was the slightest chance he might refer to the fortune she had tucked away.

"Put me down at Fifty-ninth Street, sir."

The General gave the car a kick into high gear to be the quicker shed of her, and not another word was said between them.

Mrs. Norris took the BMT, and the moment she descended the subway steps she felt her mood improve. She should not allow the old gentleman to so annoy her. He did it deliberately. She settled in the waiting car and gave herself up to watching all the mad people of New York sprinting from one train across the platform to another. She made bets with herself at every express stop. Once she had so forgot herself as to cry out: "Half a bob on him in the red socks!" It had got her into conversation with a Yorkshireman who was, alas, on his way to Kansas City. She sighed now, remembering him. His last words had been: "I hope we meet again, lass!" Many a long year it had been since anyone called Annie Norris lass, and the truth when she faced it was that except for her squabbles with the General there was very little excitement in her life any more. Ah, but that would change with Master Jamie's going back into public life. She began to think of ways she could hint at the matter to her sister without violating the confidence.

Her brother-in-law, whom she always called Mr. Robinson was, to her surprise, home when she arrived. And it was much to her pleasure. He was ever a cheerful man, where her sister Mag seemed given more every year to complaining.

Mr. Robinson took her coat and said into her ear: "You've roses still in your cheeks, Annie, never mind the frosty pow."

"The frosty pow," she repeated, running her hand over the white strands of her hair. "You're handsome as ever yourself, Mr. Robinson. It's the ride in the car—in the Jaguar if you please—that flushed my cheeks."

"Is it paid for yet?" said Mag.

And somehow Mrs. Norris resented the question although she was herself responsible for the information. "We're doing very nicely in the family, Mag. And there are certain omens in the wind that we may soon be doing better."

"Oh-ho?" said Mr. Robinson, pulling his chair closer to Mrs. Norris. "Would it be the young one or the old bird that's bringing that to the nest?" There was something in his question and his way of asking it too direct for Mrs. Norris' tastes, and her brother-in-law saw it immediately himself. "Aren't you going to give your sister a cup of tea to warm her?" he cried to his wife.

"You're home at a queer hour, Mr. Robinson," Mrs. Norris said.

"How else would I get to see you?" he said with a wink. Was it, Mrs. Norris wondered, that she was getting old and skeptical? That wink seemed to have been a strain on Mr. Robinson. For the first time in all the years of their acquaintance she doubted the sincerity of his cheerful banter. And look at Mag; she was wrinkled as a bag of cheese while he was blooming. But after a while, Mr. Robinson bringing out a bottle of what he called "Boggy Dew," Mrs. Norris thought it was all in her imagination.

"I remember," said Mr. Robinson when the drink was down, "your old gentleman was talking of writing his memoirs. Lively enough wouldn't you say they might be?"

"Lively enough to shame us all," said Mrs. Norris.

"You don't tell," said Mag, with her first pep of the day.

"He's been reading them to her," said Mr. Robinson with a wink.

"He's neither reading nor writing them, thank God for our respectability."

"Sometimes," said Mag, wrinkling her nose with disappointment, "I wonder if your respectability hasn't got in the way of your chances."

Mrs. Norris squared her shoulders. "My chances of what, pray?"

"Oh, for the love of heaven, don't be starting to snipe at

each other. Wouldn't the two of you like to go to a motion picture?" Mr. Robinson put his hand in his pocket.

"It might improve our dispositions," Mag said forlornly.

"Aw . . ." said Robbie, the twenty dollar bill already in his wife's hand, "I'm like all the victims of the con men. Get me once and you got me forever. You do this to me every time, the two of you. I must be off now." He came in again, putting on his coat. "Is it politics your old gentleman's going into, Annie?"

"Well, there's been politics in the family for generations. You know that, Mr. Robinson."

"Whatever Mr. Robinson knows or doesn't know," he said, leaning down between the two women to kiss the cheek of one and then the other of them, "the information didn't reach him by the lips of Annie Norris."

6

This was to be the General's first visit to Mr. Robinson's place of business although he had had a standing invitation for some months. His interest in the dapper little man had been first provoked by Robbie's knowledge of foreign cars which ran to such refinements as special models and the people who owned them, and then of course, there was the matter of horses, on which he was also an expert. Beyond these interests, Robbie had yet another, and that one the General had never expected to find useful to himself, English Royalty. But when he picked the printer up at the appointed hour, he came around to the subject as soon as possible.

"Do you remember telling me about your collection of royal crests and coats of arms and whatnot?"

"I remember," Robbie said.

"And charting a course to them for some obsure American descendants?"

"Was that how I put it?" said Robbie. "Oh yes, I remember. But there wasn't enough profit in printing the blasted things. And there were other complications. Ah, but I loved the research. D'you know, General, there's times I'd sooner be parted with Mag than with my books."

"You still have the books then?"

"An office full of them."

The General grunted his satisfaction. "Robbie, how would you like to help me set up a little detour in the course of history?"

"I suppose," he said, after considerable thought, "it would depend on the amount of traffic, if you know what I mean."

The General was deep in his own thoughts. "What do you suppose would have happened to the world if—say— Napolean could have slept at night? Or suppose that Russian general of cavalry had not got boils on his backside when the revolution was at its crest?"

The printer thought about the possibilities. "Do you think what happened happened because of their ills or in spite of them, General?"

The General took his eyes from the road and looked at Robbie sadly. "That is a question worthy of an Irishman. I'd not have expected it of you, Robbie. I'm reviewing the Irish parade, by the way."

"Man, man, watch the road, or you'll see it in the company of St. Patrick himself."

A few minutes later they parked in the lot at the rear of Mr. Robinson's plant, and Robbie getting out from the Jaguar, took his handkerchief from his pocket and wiped the sweat from his hands. Despite the weather, they were almost running with his nerves. He resolved to ride no more with General Jarvis in the city. He even wiped the handle of the car door where it, too, was moist from his clutching it.

Two men, watching from the doorway of the restaurant across the street, exchanged looks and ambled across the street with deliberate ease. Robbie noticed them, wondered where he had seen them before, speculated idly on whether their tans came from a gymnasium sun lamp or the Florida sun and then forgot about them.

The General's first impression of the shop was that no great amount of printing was done in it, not enough certainly to occupy the platoon of men lolling about, not one of whom seemed any more inclined to set to work on Robbie's arrival than he had been in his absence. This was not Scottish industry.

"What do they do?" he asked out.

"They're ru . . . markable men, all of them," Robbie said, steading himself after a quick change of course. If the General didn't understand what he saw, there was no need to start his education at this age. "They're messengers."

"Are they," the old man murmured.

"And this is a linotype machine," said Robbie, steering him past the one piece of equipment and into a hallway.

It needed dusting, the General thought of the machine, but he said nothing.

"Most of our work is done out," Robbie further explained, opening the door and turning the light switch in his private office. "I keep a few lads on the phone to take orders, and I have a good man on my books."

"An accountant," said the General, following his host's example and hanging his overcoat on the hall tree inside the door. Robbie looked at him sharply: the question often came up between them—who was pulling whose leg? "The most important man in our generation, Robbie, but it's not your accountant I'm interested in. I want to inquire into a certain English family of a hundred or so years ago—that of a Lady Sylvia Mucklethrop. She may have been the last of the line. I expect they're extinct by now."

"Oh, no,' said Robbie. "They're very much alive."

"Are they," the General growled. "I'd never have expected it by her taste in gentlemen." He thought about the implications of a thriving, respectable clan of Mucklethrops to his scheme. But, of course! That was better still! More's the interest.

"You'll want to look them up," said Robbie. And with that he motioned the General into a leather-upholstered chair, while he pushed a couple of buttons, one of which threw more light on what had seemed a very dismal office indeed, and the other of which turned panels as dark likely as the inside of a coffin round to shelf upon shelf of books. Robbie, with a flourish of his hand, unrolled a map and then a chart which by cross reference, he explained, would give the key to the lands and kins of many a noble family, including the Mucklethrops. Still another chart indicated the make and model of automobiles in the family. To complete the General's bewildered admiration, he opened what looked like a wall safe and brought from it a bottle of eighteen year old Scotch whiskey. He set it up with glasses.

"I have to leave you for a while now, sir. I'll be back after post time . . ."

"When?" said the General.

"After the postman goes. I have a ton of orders to get into the afternoon mail."

"Carry on," said the General, already under the British influence.

He began poking among the shelves. There were tomes on royal crests and seals, genealogies, histories and biographies, diaries and account books. It would take a librarian to sort them, and by the markings on some of the books they had once passed into and out of library hands. But that was none of the General's business. Alone in the room, or thinking himself alone, he was suddenly elated at the discovery of the name Mucklethrop. It so absorbed him that he was scarcely aware of a great lump of a fellow sweeping the office until the man swept off the tops of the General's shoes. The General bent down to look; so did the sweeper, and straightened up with him also, like a burlesque comic. The old man looked about for something to throw at him, but the fellow was gone before he found it, and all the General remembered of his looks really was that his face was the color of stage makeup.

And what a turn that gave the General, thinking of stage makeup!

Flora: it was as though his Flora had come into the room and gone from it, just while his back was turned, and not Flora as he knew her now, but as she was when first he met her. He was tempted then to pick up Robbie's phone and call her. He lifted the receiver. It was an extension phone, the line in use. He had not thought of Flora like that, in connection with the stage—for how long? Not at least since she herself had forsaken show business, and had become content in the small apartment he provided for her. He decided to let the call go since he would be seeing her that night. But he must remember to tell her. What an extraordinary experience! Like peeling twenty years from his life.

He forced himself back to his researches. "Suppose you were a Mucklethrop, Robbie," he said when the printer returned, "would it distress you to discover that your great-grandmother carried on a bit with a gentleman who was subsequently President of the United States?"

"I suppose, General," Robbie said, and after taking more time than the General thought necessary, "it would depend on where I discovered it."

"What the devil difference would that make?"

"Reliability—the reliability of the source," said Robbie. "Since you asked it, I assume you want to know."

"Go on."

"If it was true, I'd probably find it amusing. And if it was false, General, I'd sue to the depth of American prosperity."

"Oh, so would I, so would I," said the General.

"Is it the old gentleman whose picture is in your study?"

"The very same. He's been confiding to me about the Mucklethrops, Robbie," said the General slyly.

"Why, the old bastard."

The General grinned. He gave Robbie a gentle poke. "And something he's taught me: how to sign his name. Look." The General took his pen from his pocket and looped the signature, complete with its nineteenth century flourishes.

"Oh, the villain!" Robbie cried and took his handkerchief to the palms of his hands again.

"Do I dismay you?" the General asked, destroying the paper in the ashtray.

"Dismay is too mild a word. You shock hell out of me, sir."

The General gave a grunt of approval. "Before he was president, he served at the Court of St. James—this philandering ancestor of mine. He kept a diary that would put you to sleep even if you had a toothache . . . But, Robbie, he left a great blank at the end of each day's trivia as though he some day meant to enter the truth. That's what you and I are about to compose, to give to the world, and demand that history take another look at him! Is that not an honorable intent?"

"The very soul of it," said Robbie, with a bright sort of despair.

"I shall have to use a nibbed pen, of course," the General said. "Oh, there's something else I'll need. I have a formula here for ink. Do you know a chemist?"

"Kind of a chemist."

"Ring him up and engage him," the General said, and rubbed his hands together.

Robbie looked at him with admiration. "You mentioned the honorable intent of this . . . this . . ."

"Historical supplement," the General prompted. "And you would like to know the dubious intent?"

"Aye," said Robbie, "since my share likely comes out of that."

"Quite. I'm doing it for money. I expect to publish these memoirs which I, in family pride, have rescued from the dust, and to accept as my inheritance the royalties therefrom."

" 'Tis only fair," said Robbie, "but just as a matter of information, General—in case, mind only in case something gangs awry—would you still be able to draw your pension in the pokey?"

"Damn it, sir, I might as well be in the pokey now for all I see of it!"

Robbie sighed. "He jests at scars that never felt a copper's breath upon his neck."

"Oh, haven't I though? Many's the time, Robbie, many's the time, and once the breeze of a nightstick."

Robbie laughed then and the two men bent with a will to the task at hand. "I remember when I was in India," the General started. "There was a duchess of somewhere or other seated next to me at dinner one night. She came right out and said to me . . . well, actually, she whispered it, but straight, Robbie . . ."

"Oh, they're straight, the English, straight as darts. What did she say?"

The General whispered into Robbie's ear and then folded his arms. "Do you think we could use it?"

Robinson clapped his hands in pleasure. "Why not? Let me tell you, General: the Lady Mucklethrop in your President's time might as likely have said it as your duchess. 'Privilege' is an old English word, you know."

"Shall we start with that?"

"Aye, put it down, man. Put it down.

7

Since his return from Albany with the promise of the gubernatorial nomination, Jimmie had spent most of his time at the office, and he made sure that the senior partners knew it. He would have liked very much to defend in a good jury trial before summer, even if it meant a curtailment of his campaigning. Or perhaps especially if it meant such curtailment. And he belonged to a firm who still believed in going to court now and then. He was still a junior partner, however, and although it had never been so specified, he was not likely to become a senior until his father died. The old gentleman had in his youth, by leaving the firm for the military, reduced almost to permanent clerkship the Jarvis position. If there had been a younger Jarvis now in Harvard Law School, Jimmie thought . . . But there was not. In fact there was not even one in the cradle.

He was never so oppressed by this thought as at the office where women still looked out of place, where men wore vests, and where per capita there were more rimless glasses than anywhere else in the United States; he always felt himself here to be running up and down the halls of eternity. And yet, he loved the place. He would have liked very much to have become a great trial lawyer who wore his fame like a robe, to be shed on leaving the courtroom. But the pattern had been broken for him early—by the old man—who had not advocated the law for Jimmie until it seemed possible that the boy would wind up on the wrong side of it altogether. The partners still had the attitude of having taken him in to keep him out of trouble.

Still, Jimmie was only a little discontented in politics, and he wore the aura of his law firm—of all the things he thought it meant and wished it meant to him—into the political forum. That was part of his charm: his fairly modern ideas in the comfortable old shell of Victorian conservatism. Also, Jimmie thought, taking his own measure that afternoon, he had been given his childhood training by Mrs. Norris, and when in his youth it had come time for him to rebel from something, it had been from Mrs. Norris. For all he knew, that was why he had gone home to her from every woman he had known since.

Several times during the day he had thought of another woman he should call, indeed must call, to confirm their weekly date of that evening. Then the phone rang, he heard her voice and knew why he had not made the call. Helene Joyce would not suit the tastes of the party executives. But what he was going to do about it, he didn't know.

"Hello, darling," he said, "I was about to call you."

"Don't ever say that, Jimmie, even when it's the truth."

The words hit him like a blow. "Right you are, my dear."

"I don't want to be right, Jimmie. You know what I want."

And those words struck more deeply, twisting inside him the roots of longing to be with her. "Where shall we have dinner, Helene?"

She laughed softly. "I do embarrass you, don't I? I should like to go to the Ponder Inn tonight, since you've asked me."

He would have preferred dinner at her apartment, the old enchantment once again upon him. "Why there?" he said.

"Jimmie, you make the arrangements."

"Of course not, Helene. I was merely curious. I'll call for you at seven."

"Let's meet there then," she said. "I know you are to be

congratulated, and I'm sure you must be very busy. Seven-thirty at the Ponder Inn?"

"Right," he said, and looked at the phone a moment in his hand when she had hung up. How, he wondered, had she come by the knowledge of his prospective candidacy. She was not that intuitive—though damned intuitive she was.

He had met Helene ten years before—attending an exhibit of her sculpture with a friend. She had been a model in her youth, an artist's model known the breadth of Greenwich Village. Now her fame was considerably wider, international in scope. But, Jimmie thought, grimly, it would be the Greenwich Village phase of her renown which would interest the Party.

Jimmie dressed at his club and at seven-twenty-five was standing outside the Ponder Inn on East Fifty-second Street watching for Helene's cab. She was not yet late, but at the moment she should have arrived, another cab drew up. The doorman opened it and Jimmie peered in. He recognized and was recognized by Judge Turner.

The Judge emerged murmuring something like "Ah, my boy, how are you?" and Jimmie gave his hand into the cab to assist Mrs. Turner from it. It was a frail hand that took his, but the old lady smiled into his face.

"How like your father, Jimmie!" she said, leaning an instant on him to gain her balance. "But so much steadier." She squeezed his hand before releasing it.

"I don't suppose you're dining alone," the Judge said.

"No, sir," Jimmie said, but at that moment Helene arrived and he needed to introduce her. Beautiful she was, but with a lean, almost lupine sort of beauty—sensuous without being smackingly feminine. Jimmie sensed the reserve gathering in the Judge's wife.

"Mrs. Joyce," the judge repeated, not quite acknowledging or rejecting the introduction.

Jimmie's spirits sank to their lowest.

They parted, the two couples, to their separate reservations within the Ponder. For a long moment, Helene sat and looked at him, into him. Jimmie lifted his chin a little, but said nothing. When their drinks were served, Helene held up her martini and touched her glass to his. "Goodbye,

Jimmie," she said and drank a deeper draft than should be taken of a martini.

"You do take giant steps, don't you?" Jimmie said.

"I can even run when I have to," she said.

"Would you mind running into my arms before running out of them?" he said, and then rather savagely, because he was being weak in saying that: "Who the devil has been talking to you?"

Helene smiled. "Among others, the Judge's wife just now although she said not a word."

"She's an old hypocrite."

"Whatever she is, she's not that, Jimmie. And you know it as well as I do. I read in Lem Python's column—you're lunching with Madeline Barker these days."

Jimmie bristled. "She anticipates," he said.

Helene laughed. "But of course she does—that you'll be governor. I must tell you of an old association some day. Neither the best nor the worst of my youth." She was thoughtful for a moment. "If ever Madeline Barker should try to blackmail you, Jimmie . . ."

"What?" He started violently.

"I do have a dirty mind. Am I right that it's to be governor?"

He nodded.

Helene studied her glass, turning it slowly round with a strong, veined hand. She looked up at him. "Do you think you might be president some day?"

"I am not that ambitious," Jimmie said.

"You will be when the time comes," she said. "I'm very proud of you, my dear. And I shall be very circumspect. But I don't suppose that's enough, is it?"

Jimmie was saved from needing to answer another of her painful questions by the arrival at their table of the head waiter. With the menu he gave Jimmie a note, written on the back of Judge Turner's card. It read: "I will phone you at Nyack at 11 o'clock tonight."

Jimmie swore softly under his breath. On Helene's quizzical look, he gave her the card.

"I suppose," she said, "there's no question of your not being there?"

"He is, in effect, ordering me home to bed," said Jimmie.

"Alone," Helene said bluntly. She gave a great sigh. "I suppose I must tell you the story of my youth one of these days. New York is like the palm of your hand, Jimmie, millions of lines you scarcely see, but crossing and recrossing." She shrugged. "Palmistry is for the young."

Jimmie took his pen and a card from his pocket and wrote: "I'm sorry, sir. But I will not be there." He gave it to Helene to read.

She smiled and tore it up. "Shall we order dinner, Jimmie? In a way I'm grateful. My work has been suffering. You are a dreadful distraction."

A few minutes later, and when they had finally managed a conversation without strain, they were again interrupted by the head waiter. This time Jimmie was wanted on the telephone. Since the only person who knew where he was—aside from Judge Turner—was the valet at his club, someone had been at considerable pains to find him. He excused himself and took the call in the manager's office.

Mike Zabriski was on the phone. There had been a leak all right on what had gone on at Albany, and furthermore to where it could hurt most, according to Mike: the opposition was going into Jimmie's record as District Attorney.

"Let them," Jimmie said irritably. "It's clean."

"You're talking to old Mike, young fella, nobody's record is that clean."

"Yes, sir," Jimmie said.

"The way I heard it just now, for example, you made a great hoopdedoo in the papers back in the 'forties, and all the time was pushing a deal so that Johnny Rocco would just move out of your yard into Brooklyn."

"That is fantastic," Jimmie said.

"To tell the truth, son, I don't remember you prosecuting The Rock, and I don't think you needed extradition papers for Brooklyn."

"I needed cooperation, that's what I needed . . . sir."

"All right, young fella, but if I was you I'd think up the names of the people who were supposed to cooperate with you and didn't. We may need 'em. Seems like the present regime is doggone cooperative. They're out in Brooklyn now trying to pick up The Rock for questioning."

"I hope they find him," Jimmie said.

Mike's sigh into the phone came like the sound of the sea in a conch. "The Rock's an old man. He ought to have enough by now to retire to Florida, and you know, Jimmie—I wish he would. Goodnight, son."

What the Party needed, Jimmie thought, was to retire its old time hacks like Mike Zabriski. He looked at his watch. Almost nine already. Within the hour he would have to start for home. As far as he was concerned at the moment, the Judge, too, was past retirement age.

When he got back to the table, Helene was gone. The head waiter held his chair. "Madame did not wait for dessert. She said you would understand."

Jimmie glowered in the direction of the Judge's table. He and Mrs. Turner were also gone.

"The Judge?" asked the waiter discreetly. Jimmie nodded. "They exchanged a few words together, leaving."

"Did they leave together?"

"I wouldn't say that, sir. I got the impression—mind you, I may be wrong—but it is my deduction that he did not want to be present when you returned and found your companion gone."

"It's a damned good deduction," Jimmie said.

The waiter clicked his heels. "Thank you sir."

8

The General and Robbie had long since arrived at the authentic family affiliations of all whom the "diarist" proposed to make famous. And now, awaiting the return of Robbie's chemist, they were turning the spirited events of their creation into rather dull affairs by converting them into the President's style. It would be a fine irony, the General thought, if the old bore managed even at this distance to blunt the prickle of scandal. Remarkable, he complained to Robbie, what a bad cook could do to good meat.

This brought their consideration to the dinner hour, and Robbie thought it best to bring in sandwiches since there was no telling when his chemist friend would return. The Geneal grumbled about his digestion, the simplicity of the ink formula, and his need of another drink. The drink Robbie provided, and himself got into his overcoat to go for the sandwiches. He stuck his hand in his pocket, and along with his gloves pulled out a wallet. He was a minute looking at it, taken by surprise, and then opened it to the identification.

"You're getting careless with your fortune, man," he said, and tossed the wallet on the desk to the General. "You must have put it in my pocket instead of your own."

The General instinctively put his hand to the pants' pocket in which he normally kept his wallet. It was empty, at least of the wallet, but he found instead a piece of notepaper.

"I'm off," said Robbie. "I'll not be long."

The General merely nodded. He unfolded the paper and took a three-line typewritten note to the light. He read:

> I want a piece of your little plum. Make arrangements while you are there tonight or I will make them for you. You are an old man. There is enough for both of us.
>
>   Nick Casey

The name also was typed. The General sat down heavily. He might have taken his wallet from his pocket during the afternoon, but as sure as he spent the day in consciousness, he had not taken off his clothes to give anyone the opportunity of putting the note in his pocket. Nor did he put the wallet in Robbie's pocket. And at first the message made no sense to him at all. Except that the name Nick Casey was vaguely familiar.

"I want a piece of your little plum . . . tonight . . ." Flora? Did it mean Flora? But of course it meant Flora! Memory and comprehension smote him. He sat very still, commanding himself to beware of anger. At his age it could be his greatest enemy.

How well he remembered Nick Casey now! A few years ago when he returned from Europe and was spending his first evening with Flora—during the Kefauver crime hearings it was—she had gone down to the delicatessen and brought up along with the groceries a tabloid newspaper. And there was Casey's picture. "Just look at him," said Flora, and not without admiration. "Imagine, I went to public school with him. He gave me my first job. In Coney Island it was and now he owns all kinds of places in Jersey."

And of course! The oaf pushing the broom over his shoes, a nimble-fingers, a pickpocket in Casey's employ! Likely he just walked in. How would Robbie know one man from another with the motley assortment he had in the place?

"Enough for both of us!" the General cried aloud in agony, quoting the note. The vulgar, uncouth, arrogant villain!

The General had got some hold on himself by the time Robbie returned. And Robbie was now given also to thoughtfulness; had the General been less absorbed in his own problem, he might have seen it. He would have mentioned the whole matter to his friend, but what gentleman could made such a distasteful disclosure, and of so personal an affair? He and Robbie ate their sandwiches in respect for each other's silences. Finally, the chemist, a Mr. Chipsey, arrived.

He was, and even the General noticed it, a very nervous man. The General gathered his papers into his dispatch case, and put on his coat, feeling the alarm in the air.

"You know the place is bein' cased, Robbie," Mr. Chipsey said.

"Is that what those men are doing?" said Robbie, in so pious a tone even the General looked round at him.

"And you know whose boys they are, don't you?"

"No."

"Nick Casey's. Imported from Florida, so something's up."

"Nick Casey's," Robbie repeated. "I've been told they can get very nasty."

"It wasn't square of you, Robbie, to've pulled me in here, I can't afford any trouble," the "chemist" whined.

"Would I be here myself if I expected trouble? Would I have brought the General here?"

"Gentlemen, gentlemen," the General said, putting on his hat with great dignity. "I do believe Mr. Casey's interest is in myself only . . ."

"What?" Robbie shouted. "You're mixed up with Nick Casey, and come here to me like a bloody germ carrier!"

The General was always at his calmest just before zero. He turned to the other man. "Did you bring the ink, Mr. Chipsey?"

Chipsey took the bottle from his pocket. "You meant ink—when you said ink," he asked very deliberately, "didn't you?"

"Of course he did," Robbie shouted.

"You can have it free gratis," Chipsey said, and gave him the bottle.

The General decided it was no time to quibble. "Goodbye, Robbie. Wish me luck."

Robbie took his hand. "I'm sorry I spoke like I did to you, sir. You're a gentleman and a scholar."

"No, Robbie, I am a gentleman. You are a scholar."

The General moved into the hall and out the back door as against a wind. No sooner did Robbie turn the key than he switched out every light in the building. In the near darkness the General measured the distance between him and the Jaguar and just at that instant two men moved in, one on either side of him.

"Well, old man," one of them said, "what do we tell the boss?"

"Tell him it's up to Miss Tims herself," the General said. "Huh?"

The General went on, doing a bit of a dance as though their touch were loathsome to him: "If he expects to move in tonight, I shall be there, waiting for him." With that he executed a quick move whereby one thug threw the block intended for him on the other, while the General broke into the open, the Jaguar's key in his hand. He primed her with his foot and she rose as though it were a spur. In the last moment before her motor roared, the General heard men shouting; distinctly he heard: "Turn 'em loose on him, the bulls! Turn 'em loose!" The Jaguar bolted into the street. And sure enough, just before he opened the car up on the parkway, he heard the screaming of sirens. He turned east and circled west later, and was never overtaken.

9

The General did what might be called knee-dips, waiting for the elevator in the hallway of Flora's building. His legs were still shaky. It was having to drive across the Brooklyn Bridge that did it. A bridge could be a trap in these days of radio communication. Well, he had come out of it safely, whatever it was he had come out of. The elevator picked him up: it was the closest to the French type of lift he had ever seen in America, a small cage, the marvel of whose workings one could watch through the ceiling. A very appropriate sort of elevator for the house in which one kept his mistress—in the best of tradition if not of style. A feeling of serenity came upon him ordinarily in this old-fashioned contrivance—but it was missing tonight.

Whatever it was he had come out of—what was he entering into? The usual welcome of Flora's parakeet to his rap on the door did not raise his spirits. "Ransom, Ransom, Ransom," it croaked.

"I almost fell asleep, Ransom, honey. You're so late." Flora all but yawned in his face.

Greeting him thus she could scarcely have entertained Nick Casey while waiting for him, the General thought. "A bit of trouble, my dear, a bit of trouble," the General said, and kissed her cheek. "You smell delicious. Do I know it—your essence?" He gave his finger to the bird to peck at a couple of times. After that it quieted for the evening.

"Essence," Flora chided in her languid way, "they don't

call it that anymore, Ransom. That's an old fashioned word, essence."

"We're fairly old fashioned people, you and I, Flora." He looked at her critically. "You aren't dieting again, are you?"

Flora sat on the back of a chair. "I never knew a more observant man in my life. I just haven't been feelin' very well, Ransom." The drawl crept into her voice.

She had not in all these years of his telling her that he loathed the false accent she put on, realized that he really meant it, that whatever she hoped to wheedle from him thereby would be harder to get for it, not easier. Still, maybe she was right. She got what he could give her, one way or the other, and the drawl was her notion of charm, skill, witchery. It was something she could tote up in a personal assessment.

"Come tell me about it, Flora," he said, and held his hand out to her.

She sat on the arm of his chair and stroked his hand. Then she gave a great sigh. "I suppose I got to expect it, Ransom, but I get so blue and lonesome."

"Lonesome," he mimicked her pronunciation. "I received a communication today from an old flame of yours—one, I hope, my dear, you'll put out promptly."

"Tell me about it," Flora said languidly.

"I suppose you've given him no encouragement?"

"I don't know if I have or not, Ransom," she said in a schoolgirl fashion that touched his anger, "since I don't know who you're talkin' about."

"I'm talking about Nick Casey, Flora."

Her whole face blossomed into the smile. "Was Nick enquirin' after me, Ransom?"

"That is a quaint way of putting it, to say the least."

"Nick Casey," she mooned. "What does he look like now? Is he handsome still? When we were in public school, Ransom . . ."

"I know," he cut her off rudely. "It's a charming story." He took his hand from hers and caught her chin between his thumb and forefinger. "When did you see him last?"

"In person?" Flora queried.

"He's a gangster, woman, not a movie star! Yes, in person."

Flora sighed and her eyes were wistful. "It was so long ago, my hair was natural. But he gave me a job in one of his clubs."

There was something very wrong, the General thought. He wanted to read the note again now, but not in front of her. So he suggested that they have a drink and Flora went to the kitchenette for ice. He re-read Casey's note and was no wiser. "I want a piece of your little plum." The President's diary? It could not be. The scheme was no further along than the vision in his mind. Unless Casey had been listening when he sketched the plan to Robbie. Impossible. No more than a half-hour intervened between Robbie's departure from his private office and the oaf's appearance. No, no, no. The diary was too subtle a business for Casey. "Face it—you are old man . . ." Damn his insolence.

Flora returned, the tray nicely set with napkins, glasses, ice and whiskey. She had been, all in all, a wonderfully responsive girl, amenable to all the social improvements, to civilization in fact, and otherwise, marvelously uninhibited.

"What did you tell him about me, Ransom?"

For the moment he had forgotten Casey. "Oh . . . that you were a little plumper than when your hair was natural, and that I loved every ounce of it . . .

"Ransom!"

He touched his glass to hers. "How would you like to go on a vacation—away from all this?"

"Away from here?" she interrupted, and shook her head. "I'd be lost."

"With me, even?"

"I guess especially with you," she said thoughtfully.

He could understand it, he decided after a moment. This was the world she had made for him. She was its hostess, its goddess, its keeper of the flame . . . Oh, he was sentimental tonight. "If I were to make quite a sum of money soon, Flora, what would you like most?"

"I guess I would like best to have the bank book for it," she said.

The General chuckled. He went to the phone then, taking his address book from his pocket. He dialed a number, and waiting an answer, blew a kiss to Flora. With her ruddy cheeks, she belonged in a French salon, by God, he thought, with her shoulders bare, her bosom . . . "Hello, Fowler? Ransom Jarvis speaking. How are you?"

The man at the other end asked if he could call the General back in a few minutes. The General gave him the number, hung up the receiver but held the phone in his hand while he waited. "You know, Flora, how some people cannot look you in the eye while talking to you?" She nodded, "Here's a fellow that way on the telephone, believe it or not. No matter what hour you call him, at home or at the office, he must call you back. He needs to pretend that he's that busy. Sometimes I wonder if he pretends it to himself as well."

"It takes all kinds," Flora said. She came behind the General and brushed beneath his jaw with her cool fingers. "Who is he, Ransom?"

"An agent, a literary agent." As the General had expected, the phone rang within a minute. "Look, Fowler," he said, "I have a literary property I think you might like to place—what? . . . . No, not my memoirs. I'll be at them soon. This is something interesting . . ."

They made a date for ten the next morning. The General hung up the phone and looked at his watch. It was a few minutes past ten. He was suddenly very tired. Despite the note in his pocket, he was beginning to doubt the seriousness of Nick Casey's threat.

"Ransom, when you write your memoirs, am I goin' to be in them?"

He pulled her down on his lap. "I'm afraid I'm going to have to keep you hidden away in my heart forever," he said.

She was slow in speaking and her eyes came round to his slowly, as she pushed away from him. "I don't really mean much to you, do I, Ransom?" she said, and he had never seen so venomous a look. "Just somethin' you pick up once in a while like a toy doll."

"A damned expensive toy," he blurted out. "Oh, Flora, what the devil's the matter with you?"

She began to pace the room. "I don't like bein' a toy, even an expensive one!" There was something to Flora he had never known, the General thought. But of course he should have known it, the strain of panther in her. He watched the sly sensuousness of her movement.

He threw back his head and laughed. "Come here, Flora! I never loved you as well, my girl!"

She stopped and whipped the trail of her negligee from where it had twisted around her ankles. The garment fell open and she was very nearly naked. "If I come, it's not because I'm lovin' you, but 'cause I'm owin' you."

The General dropped his eyes. He got up slowly and put on his overcoat without a word. They had had quarrels before, but never on this level. There was but one answer, she no longer needed him. Nick Casey was not so far away, after all. Flora flung herself on the studio couch then, face down, and began to weep. A really sordid scene, the General thought, adjusting his hat in the mirror. He did not want to seem to hurry, but he felt a certain urge for haste, nonetheless. There was not much point in his being heroic when their affairs had come to such a pass. He started violently at the ringing of the doorbell. Flora too started up. The parakeet made such a racket, she needed to throw the sheet over it on her way to the house phone.

"I think it's Nick Casey," she said, her hand over the mouthpiece. But automatically she was pressing the buzzer to admit him.

"Is there any other way for me to leave here?" the General demanded.

Flora nodded, waving to the window. "The fire escape."

The General tried to recall an occasion when he had been here in daylight. The window looked down on some sort of court. He sat on the windowsill and swung his legs out. She was all but pushing him.

"I'm an old man, Flora," he pretested, and for the first time in his life.

"Then hang onto the railin'," Flora said.

He caught hold of it and took his first step down. The whole contraption sagged and he came near pitching forward and down.

"Be careful, Ransom," Flora cried, and immediately closed the window between them.

His temper warmed him then to the task of his descent. It was, after all, but three floors. On the second he paused and without thinking what he was doing, stared inside. A woman looked up from where she had been polishing her toenails. She gave a scream and leaped for the phone. The General moved gingerly, and the ladder rode down to the ground beneath him. He found the passage to the street that brought him out a few feet from the building entrance. There at the door of a black limousine—double parked—waited the two lads who had tried to pick him up coming out of Robbie's.

Thank God he had put the Jaguar in a garage. He retreated into the court again and looked for another exit opposite. Finding it, he looked up at the window from which he had made his departure. She had even pulled the blind! Oh, what a dissembling witch, his Flora!

The General was making his way out of the court onto another street when he heard police sirens. Perhaps to rescue the lady with the unfinished paint job on her toenails? How would Mr. Casey feel, hearing the sirens? Would his boys drive off without him? Perhaps he too would depart via the fire escape! The General was almost tempted to wait and watch. Police cars were converging from all directions. Then he was struck with the vulnerability of his own position. He skipped out into the street, sprinted the hundred or so feet to Third Avenue and then slowed his pace. He went into the next bar for a drink. Suddenly he wiped the sweat from his forehead. It was an astounding thing, but he had come within an ace of arrest as a Peeping Tom!

10

In the morning the General fell asleep again after he had been called. He had spent the night at his club, and with a rare sense of fellowship for the men he usually thought dullards, he had stayed up too late at cards. He woke with the peal of the phone bell: "his broker's office"—that was Flora. He refused the call. He needed then to have a Turkish bath, and all in all, he was pressed for time at breakfast. He could but glimpse someone else's discarded paper and he tore from it the pages carrying two items, one of which at least he intended to fully savor later:

Nick Casey, a figure prominent during the crime hearings, had been picked up for questioning as a Peeping Tom in the courtyard of an East Side apartment. The woman who at first swore he had appeared twice on her fire escape, later withdrew the charge, when a neighbor affirmed Casey to have been with her at the time. Casey said that he had left the apartment of Miss Flora Tims in such an unconventional manner on hearing her doorbell ring. He had not wished to embarrass her, an unmarried lady.

The General made a clucking sound and stuffed the page into his pocket. And Flora had the nerve to call him at the club that morning! She had used their usual ruse, of course . . . his broker's office calling. Just the same it was crude of her.

The other item concerned Jimmie: they were out for his hide already, poor boy. The district attorneys of three counties were cooperating in the effort to pick up Johnny "The Rock" Rocco, old time rum-runner, who was wanted now for questioning about the Manhattan killing in 1948. . . . The General paused and placed the date for certain; it was during Jimmie's term all right. Oh yes, the newspaper had made the same calculation: "During the administration

of James Ransom Jarvis, an indictment was sought against
Rocco, but for reasons now under investigation, was never
brought. Jarvis, who has since served in the United States
House of Representatives, is prominently mentioned as a
likely candidate for governor this year."

Poor boy, poor boy. Well, it was the price one paid for the
privilege of public service. The General pocketed that page
also, but he put its matter out of mind for the time being. He
needed all his wits to confront Augie Fowler within the
hour.

The agent kept him waiting no longer than it took to
finish a phone call. There was rather more pomp to his
manner than usual, the General thought. He was what Mrs.
Norris would call "a weatherable man," meaning that he
could smell in the wind something to his advantage.

"By the way," he said, gesturing the General into a chair,
"you're to call your broker's office."

The General grunted his thanks. Flora, obviously, was in
a hard way to get hold of him. How canny of her, to have
found him here. That was not quite like her. "Well, shall we
get down to business?" he said.

The agent nodded. "What have you got?"

"A most extraordinary thing, Fowler, an unpublished
diary of a president of the United States."

"Which one?" Fowler said. "I mean which president."
The General named him.

"That's one I've never heard of," the agent said bluntly.

"He was unsensational—at least as the world knew him
then—my grand-uncle, by the way."

"Oh?" said Fowler with the look of first believing a word
the General said. "And you think that at this late date his
diary ought to find a publisher?"

"My dear man, it is a debt to history, on the part of the
publisher, myself and now you. Futhermore, I don't think it
would embarrass any of us financially."

"I wouldn't allow myself an opinion on that if I were
you, General. Frankly, the only kind of diary I could stir up
interest in right now—well, it would have to come out of
my lady's chamber, if you know what I mean."

"Precisely," the General said.

The agent looked at him to be sure his meaning had got across. "Okay. Let's have a look at it."

"Oh, it's far too precious to cart around. But let me read you a few passages which I have transcribed. This, you understand, occurred while he was ambassador to England. The lady in mention is of a house still prominent in English nobility, by the way . . . which I don't suppose needs inhibit us, eh?"

"Read, read," Fowler said, with an impatient wave of his hand.

The General selected a provocative passage naturally, and glimpsing an actual glint of greed creeping into Fowler's eyes as he listened, he wished that he had long long ago turned his hand to fiction.

"You know," Fowler said when the General pocketed his sample, "we could feed bits of this—without names, probably, to the columnists. Whet the public interest. It might start some bidding before ever we submit to publishers."

"My own humble sentiments," the General said, and they proceeded to discuss the length and further content of the diary. The old man listened carefully. He wanted consistency as well as flexibility for his future action. And finally, cautioning both himself and the agent, he said: "Of course we shall want to keep our dignity in this. Nothing vulgar. And I must consider Jimmie and his career."

"I was just wondering about him," Fowler said. "How does he feel about the project?"

The General shrugged. "Neither one way nor the other."

"In other words, you haven't confided your . . . discovery to him." The agent grinned. "I've not invested in your postmilitary career for nothing, General."

"It's time some of the profits went back into the firm then," the General growled. He wondered if Fowler suspected the true composition of the diary. It would be just as well if he did; he would not dare say so, and a little caution there might edit his own exuberance.

"As soon as there are profits, General. When do I get to read this book of revelations?"

"Do you want to see it in manuscript?"

"Preferably not—but someone will have to authenticate it, besides yourself."

"Of course! And someone will damn well have to pay for its transcription."

"I can probably manage that," Fowler said dryly. The General got to his feet. "It's too bad," Fowler went on, taking him to the door, "this Rocco business just now. Tell me, was Jimmie really on his way to the governor's office, or was that press agentry?"

"Jimmie Jarvis *is* on the way to the governor's office, Fowler."

"Then you don't think Rocco's murder will seriously hurt him?"

"Rocco's murder?" the General repeated.

"That's the way I heard it on the radio this morning. Seems like he got taken on an old-fashioned ride, black limousine, the works."

"A black limousine?" The General again echoed Fowler's words. His brain seemed full of lightning thoughts, and not a one he could hold onto. "I'll be in touch with you later, Fowler," he murmured, and made his way quickly out and to the street. There he bought the latest edition of the papers. The Rocco murder was headlined. He took all the papers back to his club to read.

Jibber-jabber, most of it, all middle without head or tail, showing clearly but one thing, the bias of the paper: the story was slanted against Jimmie or in his defense, but every newspaper account pointed out the connection between the gangster's murder and Jimmie's political fortunes.

It was a matter of some curiosity, the General thought, that Nick Casey owned a black limousine. And while he, the General, had seen it on Manhattan's east side after ten o'clock, he, the general, also knew that the distance between there and the Red Hook district of Brooklyn, where Rocco had been seen getting into a limousine at midnight, could be driven in less than an hour. He had done it himself not much earlier.

Very interesting.

The club lounge was filling up, the luncheon hour approaching. Another call came from his broker's office.

Flora was very persistent. This time he said he would call within the hour. He moved to a solitary place by the window. It was interesting, too, that by a strange combination of circumstances, Casey himself had the most honorable of witnesses as his whereabouts at midnight: he was in a police station pleading innocent to charges of prurient spying.

Oh yes, he must soon call Flora. But first he must call Jimmie, poor boy. The General drew a deep breath and with it caught in the fragrance of flowers. Carnations he thought, and looked about for the vase. True enough, green carnations. What a perpetration, turning to bilious green nature's loveliest bloom. But of course, tomorrow was St. Patrick's Day.

The General put through a call to Nyack. It was Mrs. Norris who answered. "Well," he said, "how did you find your family? Or better, how did you leave them?"

"You no doubt want to speak to your son," Mrs. Norris said, and it would have taken a hatchet to crack the ice in her voice. Surely Robbie had not betrayed him to her?

"Hello, father." Jimmie's voice sounded straining with tolerance.

"I'm sorry for all your trouble, my boy."

"Then maybe you'll tell me what you were doing in Brooklyn last night, father."

"Brooklyn?"

"The District Attorney's men got your licence number. They are not unreasonable in the conclusion that either you were there—or I was."

"But, but," said the General, "you have witnesses to where you were, don't you?"

"It so happens that I was home alone, here in Nyack, that I expected a phone call which I deliberately did not answer when it came."

"Oh," said the General, grabbing anything that might float him. "The phone is tapped, is it? We had better not talk then. I'll explain everything when I see you."

"The phone is not tapped!" Jimmie said, "and I don't care if it is."

"Where was Mrs. Norris when you needed *her* last night?"

"She stayed over with her sister until this morning. Father, where were you?"

"I'm sorry not to have been there, my boy. I was at my club most of the night as a matter of fact. I spent the night here. I want to help you every way I can, you understand . . ."

"All right, father, stow it. Are you going to review the parade tomorrow or not?"

"Would you doubt it? I'd march for you if I had but one leg."

"You won't have to march," Jimmie said wearily. "Now listen to me. I've engaged rooms for us at the Mulvany Hotel, adjoining rooms. We'll be right on Fifth Avenue. You can check in any time you like. I'll have Mrs. Norris pack your things and I'll bring them. Here's Mrs. Norris. Tell her what you need . . ."

" 'Tell her what you need,' " the General mimicked. He had hired her as a nurse for his son, and he was damned if he was going to have her turned into a nurse for him forty odd years later. She would right now be full of tears and self-recriminations for having let the boy down. The General could not resist giving a jab with the needle: "Your brother-in-law must have been highly entertaining last night, Mrs. Norris."

"He was not at home, sir. Indeed, it's why I stayed. My sister was very worried when he did not come home from his work till long after his usual hour."

"Could he not have called at least?" said the General, remembering the wealth of telephones in Robbie's establishment.

"I think that's a good question for all of us to ask ourselves, sir."

The General cleared his throat and named a few items she was to pack for him. Plainly he had walked into something foul yesterday, up at least to his pockets. And it was just as plain he had to get out of it quickly or else pull Jimmie in with him. He probably needed the help of a confidential investigator, and for that he needed money. He took the small bag of toilet essentials he kept at the club with him, got his dispatch case from the safe, looked to be sure the diary and ink were in it, and went to the Mulvany Hotel. The hotel arrangement was fine: a private club was not private enough for some transactions.

He debated with himself while waiting the preparation of his room, which of his calls to make first and decided on Fowler. Having a dime, he made the call from a public phone. He caught the agent on his way out to lunch, and came directly to the point: "Augie, for one thousand dollars cash this afternoon, I am willing to sign over to you one half my interests in the diary."

There was a long pause before the agent spoke. "Where is the diary now, General?"

"I will deliver it into your hands by five o'clock this afternoon." Long before then, he thought, he could make the entries of his and Robbie's composition.

"Then I will make you a personal loan against the publisher's advance on the property, General. However, the customary ten percent of your earnings on it will satisfy me."

"You are an honest man, Augie."

"In some things I suppose I am," the agent said dryly. "See you at five."

The General decided he had better do his copy work immediately. There was an unsteadiness to his hand he did not like. With more stress it would not improve. He took a warm bath, came from it relaxed, satisfied as to his ability to do such exacting work, double-bolted the doors and set to the task. Only when it was finished did he turn to the other call he had to make. Flora seemed a very long time answering.

11

Not for a moment did Jimmie believe that the district attorneys of three counties were out to get him, and he told Mike Zabriski as much that afternoon. It was one thing to reopen an investigation for political purposes, but quite another to pin a murder on a man.

"I wouldn't say that was being done to you, young fella," Mike said.

"The afternoon papers come mighty close to it."

"Bread and butter headlines," Mike said.

"Mike, why was Judge Turner so determined to get me home by eleven last night?"

Mike rolled a protruding lower lip even lower. "I guess the Judge would be the one to answer that, Jimmie." He nodded toward the conference room adjoining his office. "Look here now, don't get any notions like that."

"Like what?"

"Like that the Judge had information that Rocco was going to be bumped off," Mike said bluntly.

"If I allowed myself to think that for an instant," Jimmie said, "I would resign—if possible from the human race itself."

"That's my brave young fella," Mike said. He was once again proud of his candidate. He pointed to the phone on his desk. "Try the General again."

Jimmie swore softly and dialed the Mulvany Hotel. It was the third time he had tried to reach his father, having had to go himself directly to Mike's office to a Party executive conference. Again the hotel switchboard reported that General Jarvis was not taking any calls. What really worried Jimmie was that his father might have been trapped into some sort of complicity either by flattery or the lure of

money; he was always in great need of both. Jimmie shook
his head.

"I don't see much point in doing anything till you get that
straightened out," Mike said.

"There's one thing needs to be found out if they don't
already know it," Jimmie said, "what Rocco has been
doing lately."

Mike nodded his head ponderously. "I guess you know
I've got an informant in the D.A.'s office?"

"I know such characters exist," Jimmie said. He knew
damn well Mike had inside information.

"It's a funny sort of business they haven't really got hold
of—it looks like he's been running a protection racket for
bookies."

Jimmie whistled. "No wonder they haven't got hold of it.
It's too hot." After all, who did bookies need most
protection from? The police. Jimmie got up and rubbed his
hands together. "Mike, do you know what I'm going to do?
I'm going to offer my services as a special investigator to
the D.A.'s office." Mike nodded approval. Jimmie asked:
"What do you say we give that to the newspapers?"

"Better see first what comes out of this meeting," Mike
said, getting up, checking his watch, and leading the way
into the conference room.

A hasty session of the Party executives in New York at
the time had been called. They sat now, their eyes
downcast. Jimmie wondered if he would be ditched there
and then. But all that happened was that a policy chairman,
pro tem, was elected, through which activities and news
releases affecting the party must be cleared. In other words,
Jimmie thought, from now on, he must live as though even
moths and flies had camera eyes. How poetic a thought! His
champion of the hour was Madeline Barker. And since, as
well, she was put in nomination by Mike for the chairman-
ship, and the move to close nominations was made by the
Judge, Jimmie certainly could not oppose her. But he
remembered well her behavior at Albany. And Helene's
remark about blackmail . . . he had not had the chance to
pursue that. Well, she might be a fragile Barker—Miss
Madeleine, but she had got herself a convoy of some mighty
sturdy old men-of-war.

She approved his offering of his services to the District Attorney, but with one qualification: "unless your father—the old dear—is implicated."

If his father—the old dear—was implicated, Jimmie swore, taking a cab crosstown to the Mulvany, he intended to know it within the hour. The bags he had sent ahead were already in his and the General's rooms. The old dear had answered his bell for that all right. Jimmie watched the clerk get him the key to 517. He was about to turn away when he saw the key lying in the next box. "Doesn't my father have room 519?"

"Yes, sir," the clerk said, glancing at the box. "The General seems to be out at the moment."

"Without leaving a message for me?"

"I'm afraid so, sir."

"Or word as to when he would return?"

"No, sir, no word at all."

The villainous rogue, Jimmie thought, and then tried to restrain his judgment until he reached his own room and looked to see if there were a message under the door there. But there was none.

Jimmie looked at his watch. It was almost five. He would have liked very much to get on with his investigative offer today, so he sat down to sweat out his father's return. When the General had not returned by six, Jimmie called his club. He was not there. As seven Jimmie called Mrs. Norris. She had not heard from him. Jimmie promised to call her back. By eight o'clock Jimmie's anger was being tempered by concern. The more he thought about it, the more he realized how little he knew of his father's activities. He was reasonably sure the old man had a mistress, but both he and his father respected each other's privacy. It was, Jimmie thought grimly, the only possible way they could live together. He wondered then if Mrs. Norris would know. She knew a good many things she considered unmentionable. He called her again.

"Do you think he has a friend he might be with?"

"A female friend?" Mrs. Norris asked.

God, Jimmie thought, but the English language was ugly when used like a blunt instrument. "That's what I had in mind," he said.

"If I have your permission I'll go through his things and call you back," she said.

Jimmie thought of his father's wrath at the discovery of that exploration. "I don't think I'd better be a party to that, Mrs. Norris."

"Now and then," Mrs. Norris said, "I've taken a call to him from a woman who said it was his broker's office calling. I think it was her called this morning. Remember, I told you? She hung up when I said he wasn't home."

"I remember," Jimmie said dully. It was a matter he would have to drop there. "Did he take you to Brooklyn yesterday?"

"He did not. I thought of that myself when I heard he was there. He didn't want us to know where he was going."

"And obviously he doesn't want us to know where he is now," Jimmie said. "All right, Mrs. Norris. I'll call you later."

"Mr. Jamie?"

"Yes."

"Have you eaten your dinner?"

"Not yet."

"You go out of that room this minute and have a nice warm meal. Mind me, now."

"I suppose you're right," Jimmie said. "I can go downstairs and have them page me if he comes in."

"Do. And something digestible. Not too fancy."

But Jimmie was not paged throughout his dinner which he did his best to linger over, because the prospect of waiting in his room was too terrible. In fact, leaving the dining room at a quarter to ten, he made up his mind that he would have to take some action if he had not heard from his father by eleven. Jimmie stopped at the desk again. The Mulvany was a small hotel, elegant and intimate, such as had all but disappeared from New York, and it was very, very proper. There was suddenly a severe aloofness on the part of the clerk. Instinctively, Jimmie looked at the key box, room 519. His father's key was not in it.

Jimmie all but exploded. "Is General Jarvis in his room?"

"He is, sir," the clerk said frostily.

"I asked to be informed . . ."

"I beg your pardon, sir, you asked to be paged if he called. He was in no condition to speak to you, sir. Out of consideration for you, and our other guests, I thought it best to have him taken directly upstairs. He abused me horribly."

"That's some satisfaction," Jimmie murmured, and started for the elevator. "What time did he come in?"

"An hour ago, perhaps," the clerk said, glancing at his watch.

He would never be governor, Jimmie decided in the elevator. Wherever he found them, he must call stupid men stupid, and all of them had the vote. Or, perhaps, thus would he come to office! When the only justice was poetic. He knocked on the door of 519. No answer. "Father, I've had enough nonsense," he said, trying to make his voice carry without raising it. He knocked harder on the door. Still no answer. He tried the door. It was locked. He went around to the door of the bathroom which they shared. He hammered and all but kicked it in. To no avail. He called the desk then and asked the clerk to send up the pass key to 519, and when the clerk protested, Jimmie suggested that he send the house detective along with him; the old gentleman might have had a heart attack.

He went out in the hall to wait. The house detective came, put his key in the lock and glanced up at Jimmie. If the door had been locked from the inside, the key was not in it. The detective turned his passkey, withdrew it, and gestured Jimmie to proceed.

Jimmie threw the door open. The detective shone the beam of his flashlight about the darkened room. It caught the old man. He was awkwardly slumped over the back of a chair, as though he were hanging onto it, and yet in such a position that gravitation would seem to demand that he fall.

Jimmie ran to him while the detective turned on the wall switch, flooding the room with light. The minute Jimmie touched him, the old man tumbled to the floor. He was dead.

Dead, Jimmie marveled, wearing all the decorations befitting his rank and service. It was as though he had come upstairs and prepared himself for the next day's duties before allowing himself to die.

12

Though he bear the shame of it to his own grave, Jimmie had to admit to himself at least that, listening to the house detective call the Medical Examiner's office, his first thought was: it's too much to expect of General Jarvis, a plain, simple heart attack.

Everyone, without saying so to him, seemed to share the view; men came from Homicide and precinct headquarters. Royalty could not have turned out more press representatives. Jimmie was glad, however, to see George Fallon, the District Attorney, and even more pleased to see in his company, his chief investigator, Jasper Tully, whom Jimmie trusted. Tully had served under him and many a D.A. before him and after him: he was forever shuffling his politics— easily shaking out the jokers for the next deal. A long, lean melancholy man, he had never to Jimmie's knowledge raised his voice, though many a man he had set to screaming by his silent scrutiny.

Jimmie shook his hand affectionately and then turned to the D.A. "You know, Fallon, I was only waiting to talk to my father, tonight. Then I intended to volunteer my services . . . on the Rocco business."

"Looks like charity can begin at home now, doesn't it?" Fallon said, and then bethought himself that he was speaking to the dead man's son. "Sorry, Jarvis, but damn it, man, we were waiting, too. Just to give you the chance to make the first move. We purposely quashed the information that your father got in our line of fire last night, and that's trouble for us in some quarters, sitting on something worth a headline."

"Thanks," Jimmie said. It struck him then that the old man would not again get into anyone's line of fire, and the blow hurt.

Tully understood. "He was always a swell target, the General." He laid a bony hand on Jimmie's shoulder.

Jimmie gave him a wink and squared his shoulders. "Let's talk some cold facts, gentlemen, just we three. I don't know what my father was doing in Brooklyn—if he was there. Now I'll have to take your word for it. I'd feel a lot better about that if I knew the full story on why the sudden interest in Johnny, The Rock. The truth, Fallon: was it politics?"

Fallon, not much older than Jimmie, pursed his lips. "When you were in my shoes, Jarvis, would you have answered a question like that?" He didn't wait for Jimmie's answer. "I don't mind telling you most of the truth. Won't give you names though. A couple of public investigators, we'll call 'em, wanted to dig through the records. I've let people with poorer credentials search them. I knew by the dates what they were after, but I'll tell you something, Jarvis, it hit both Tully and me between the eyes when they came up with the name Johnny Rocco. Johnny's had his name bantered around a lot in our circles lately on account of some very large bookmaking. In Brooklyn, true. But that's not far enough away for us to relax. They've been pulling raids regularly over there, the D.A.'s men, and getting peanuts. Peanuts for the monkeys. Now you and I know that no good cop likes to be made a monkey out of. Comprenez?"

Jimmie nodded. He had got the same story from Mike: the suspicion of the police themselves. "That's bad stuff," he said.

"That it is. So you can see, Jarvis, how it was that when they said 'sick 'im' to me, I put my best hound dog on the trail. It was your friend Tully here who spotted your father last night. He was working out of the Brooklyn D.A.'s office. Fill it in from there, Jasp. I'd like to hear it again myself. Maybe it'll make sense this time."

Tully gathered in his legs and folded his hands. You could perish waiting for his first word, Jimmie thought. "The D.A. had a couple of leads over there, so when I showed up to help they decided to stake 'em out last night. Three of their boys and me were posted outside a little one-arm restaurant called Minnie's on Water Street."

"What time?" said Jimmie.

"We set up about seven, figuring the collector would show before ten o'clock. And after the first hour we were dead sure we had something: in all that time one customer. Two roast beef sandwiches he took out with him. So we just sat, four of us outside, Minnie inside."

"Do they always go in fours over there?" Jimmie asked.

"I don't know that, but there was a couple too many of us all right as it turned out. The car wasn't marked, and there was other cars, but this round-faced goon sure spotted us. It went off like a string of firecrackers. This fellow was coming to us on the run, don't know where from, we picked up the sound of his feet hitting cement first, and I knew at the same time there was a car coming fast. When I open the window this cheese face hollers: 'You want Johnny Rocco? Go get him!' He was shouting because just about then the Jaguar goes by like a Jet out of hell. Our driver had his foot on the accelerator, but we never got any closer than the minute I got the license number, and it hit me right then maybe the car was the decoy, and the moon-faced guy the real collection man. By the time we got back he was gone, of course. Keystones, bloody Keystone cops they made of us."

Jimmie could see the famous melancholia settling on Jasper.

"It was routine I put a tracer on that license number, Jimmie. I knew it was RO—Rockland County; in fact that's what made me think we'd been decoyed." Jasper scratched his ear. "Funny, RO—Rockland County. Ro, Rocco. He was a great guy for sport cars, too. He left a sweet little Austin-Healey in front of the bank last night."

Jimmie thought about those implications. "You never picked up The Rock's trail at all then?"

"Nope. Not till we saw him on a slab in the morgue this morning."

"Do you suppose your father could have been used as the decoy, Jarvis?" the D.A. asked.

"Goddamn it," Jimmie exploded, "he was a general in the United States Army!"

"Maybe he was covering up for somebody who got in trouble," Tully said softly. "There's a lot of times respectable people get mixed up with mobsters. Say they like the horses. Did he have lots of money?"

Jimmie held up his hands. "If my father had owned the state of Texas, gentlemen, he could still have managed to be out of funds by any given weekend. That is why, unfortunately, I have to speak slowly when I defend him."

"How is Mrs. Norris?" Tully asked, having a sudden association with someone who also spoke slowly when it came to defending the General.

"She'll be in tonight, I expect," Jimmie said. He looked at his watch. "Eleven-twenty. It's taking them a while in there, isn't it?"

Both men shrugged, as though casualness best explained it.

"Finish up your Brooklyn fiasco for us, Jasper," Fallon said.

Tully looked at him mournfully. "Well, it wasn't ten minutes till we got back to Minnie's. Minnie never saw or heard of Moon-Face, of course. Matter of fact, I never did either. I went through the gallery today and I couldn't find him. Anyway, it wasn't another fifteen minutes till Minnie closed up and went home. That was twenty minutes to nine. And he did go home, I dropped out and tailed him myself all the way to his television set.

"I picked up the boys in front of Rocco's house later. In fact all four stakeouts wound up there at midnight. At three o'clock we knocked off. Eight hours of nothing. And just about that time the beat man patrolling the First Federal Bank on Fulton Street came on the Austin-Healey at the curb, motor still running. He checked the bank, nothing happening. Went back, turned off the ignition. Forgot about it. They're going to give him a wooden medal tomorrow. And here's another nice touch: at seven-fifty this morning his relief man ticketed the car for illegal parking."

"Where did the papers get the 'black limousine'?" Jimmie asked.

"A drunk claims to be a witness. He was sitting in the precinct station when it broke this morning. Said he tried to tell a cop about the guy he saw being shoved into the black limousine on the same corner, near the bank last night. Even gave the cop the license number, nice simple number, Jersey license plate. The only trouble, he must've juggled the numbers. No such combination issued."

"Son of a gun," said Jimmie.

"I said something like that myself when I heard it," Tully said.

13

One hour and twenty-one minutes after hanging up the phone in Nyack, Mrs. Norris flailed her way through policemen and reporters to the desk of the Mulvany. The taxi had cost her ten dollars and she had made the driver earn it. In the moment's politeness she now allowed herself before interrupting, she realized that the clerk was accounting to the police the General's staggering state of inebriation.

"That's a lie!" she said without thinking, but with a poke of her umbrella for emphasis.

"Were you here, madam?" The clerk looked at her ferociously.

"Were you in his employ for over forty years?" she snapped back.

"Certainly not, thank God. But I tell you, Officer, he staggered in here on the arms . . ."

"Young man! I don't believe your generation knows the difference between a stagger and a swagger." She addressed herself to the policeman with the notebook then. "I assure you, Officer, General Jarvis never staggered in his life, not

once since he got out of rompers." And to the clerk again:
"What's the room number?"

"Five-nineteen. But you can't go . . ."

"Ah, but I can," she said, and did. She was passed from
the door of the General's room, however, to Jimmie's, and
there Jasper Tully admitted her. Jimmie rose to meet her,
and caught her in his arms when she lunged at him like a
tumbling sack of potatoes. "The poor old gentleman," she
said, and meant it.

Jimmie introduced her to the District Attorney, Fallon,
and then asked, "Do you remember Jasper Tully?"

Tully pulled himself to his best height.

"Most of him," Mrs. Norris said, needing to lift her head
to look into his face.

The men laughed, but Mrs. Norris looked at Jimmie
solemnly. "And to die a spectacle in a public place," she
said under her breath.

"Now that's not quite so, Mrs. Norris. As a matter of
fact, father came upstairs and somehow managed to bedeck
himself in full regalia for tomorrow's review. There's
something rather desperately heroic about that, isn't there?"

"Ah, lad, he was a good man when it came to his
country. Did he have his medals?"

Jimmie nodded and Mr. Tully pulled at the lobe of his ear,
a habit he had at moments of registering something to
remember.

It was not long then until the Medical Examiner came in.
He had found nothing to indicate that the General had not
died from a coronary attack, but in view of the hotel
employee's account of his drunkenness—Jimmie and Mrs.
Norris exchanged glances on this—he thought an autopsy
was indicated. It would show the justified degree of
intoxication, and as well it would reveal if anything in the
nature of a drug had been administered to him. At this Mrs.
Norris nodded her head in approval, unseen by anyone save
Tully.

Jimmie agreed entirely. The funeral would be set for
Monday. Meanwhile, he agreed also that it was best for the
police to give the General's room the usual treatment where
there is a chance of murder, especially since the two

unidentified people who had brought him home, a man and a woman, had accompanied him upstairs. It was decided also, that since there was an accommodation available, Mrs. Norris should stay the night at the Mulvany.

Mr. Tully then addressed himself to her: "While the boss and Mr. Jarvis are winding up their business, would you do me the pleasure of a cup of tea and a bit of talk?"

"I would dearly love the cup of tea," she said bluntly. In the elevator, she tried to remember what she could of the detective from Jimmie's days as his superior. "Do you still live in the Bronx, Mr. Tully?"

"I do," he said, pleased that she remembered. "With my sister, you know, me being a widower fifteen years."

"Ha!" she said. "I'm widowed over forty years myself. A sailor he was, lost at sea."

The elevator operator looked around at them.

"Keep your eyes on your buttons," Tully said. The elevator drew to a stop. "Were you that curious, young man, when you took General Jarvis upstairs?"

"I didn't take him, sir."

"Somebody else on duty?"

The boy bit his lip a moment as though debating the advisability of the truth. He plunged into it. "You see, sir, there weren't many people in the lobby. It's the lull between dinner and after theatre at that hour, and just as they were getting into the elevator, right there by the ashstand—"he pointed to the stone jar of sand a few feet before them—"I saw a bill, a two dollar bill it turned out. I stuck the rod in the door and went to pick it up. Maybe a minute was all 'There's another one,' the fellow says, and I looked around. They were in the elevator by then, you see, and before I knew what was happening, he says, 'Never mind, sonny. I'll take it up."

"Sonny," Jasper repeated.

"I don't know why he called me that, sir." The boy was over six feet.

"Because you're so bright," Tully said. "I suppose you had to walk up to the fifth floor then and get your machine?"

"Yes."

"And they were out of sight by then?"

"No, sir. They were just going into the room, and I spoke out: 'You shouldn't ever do that, sir. It's not allowed.' Something like that, I said."

"Did he answer you?"

"I don't know whether you could call it an answer or not. He made a dirty gesture."

Tully gave an almost imperceptible wink to Mrs. Norris, but he pulled a longer face on the operator. "Did you bring them down later?"

"No, sir. They must have left when I was on my relief—or walked."

"What did they look like?"

Someone upstairs wanted down and the buzzer sounded. "The woman was fiftyish. I could smell her perfume in the elevator. Kind of beat-up pretty. Blond. He was strong looking, bossy, quick."

"What would you say he did for a living?"

"Circus maybe. I better go up, sir. Maybe he was a fight trainer. May I go or I'll be reported?"

"Let me have your two dollar bill," Tully said.

"I'd like to keep it for a souvenir," the boy said.

Tully put his hand in his pocket. "Here's a three dollar denomination. It's better. They aren't making them any more."

The young man was almost through the exchange before he realized that he was being ribbed. "Wise guy," he said, "sir!"

Mr. Tully put his hand beneath Mrs. Norris' elbow and steered her toward the drugstore. It was the only place of non-alcoholic refreshment open at that hour. "Kind of beat-up pretty," he murmured, "sweet smelling. Like a stepped-on rose, I guess."

The brightness of the chromium-streamed shop was a shock after the sedate softness of the Mulvany's lobby lights. Mr. Tully ordered tea for two with a double order of tea bags, and sat opposite her in a booth. He had to apologize for knocking into her with his bony knees. His legs were hard to arrange in close quarters. And looking into his deeply lined face, Mrs. Norris wondered if ever she had seen a man so homely.

"Lost at sea, was he?" Mr. Tully said then. "Well, it's a clean grave and deep, as my mother used to say."

"Was she Irish?" Mrs. Norris inquired.

"She was."

"The Irish have a great fear of shallow graves," she observed.

"That's a fact," he admitted, and thought about it—or something else. He was not a man to rush a phrase. Their tea came then. "I suppose it's because it's a stony country. A drop or a squeeze, Mrs. Norris? Milk or lemon?"

Oh, there was a devil in him. "Neat," she said.

And a little twitch trembled his eyebrow. "Am I wrong in thinking you would debate the General's being drunk?"

"Him being as drunk as that prig of a desk clerk said, oh yes. I would debate that. He was a man of uncommon experience in many things, including the bottle."

Tully nodded. "Of course if he was sick now, that would be something else, wouldn't it?"

"I suppose. But he had a good hold of himself, if you know what I mean, Mr. Tully. He wasn't one to dribble his frailties like a mewling child."

Tully drank deeply of the scalding tea. He was as leathery inside as out. "And he did have a spray of eloquent abuse for the desk clerk as he accounts it," the investigator said. "A perplexing affair altogether. It wouldn't bother me half so much, you know, if the two who brought him home weren't so skittish. Would you mind sitting in while I talk with that clerk, Mrs. Norris? I don't think it would hurt a bit to give him an extra going over tonight."

14

The clerk complained of having already told his story to the precinct men and a man from Homicide. Also, he was due to have gone off duty an hour before, having come on at noon.

"Then you were here when General Jarvis checked in," Tully remarked.

"I was."

"Sober?"

"I do not drink, sir."

Tully sighed. "Was the General sober, by those exemplary standards of yours?"

"Perfectly."

"And when he went out again, a few minutes before five wasn't it—was he sober then?"

"I was busy then, but there was nothing abusive in his manner." The young man smoothed his hair.

"So we come to the General's return—when he was abusive. Between eight-thirty and nine, and roaring drunk. Isn't that what you said?"

"Loud drunk," the clerk qualified, with a look at Mrs. Norris that seemed to credit her with the qualification.

"Could he stand up?"

"With difficulty. And his companions were almost as drunk."

"Ah yes, the companions," Tully said. They were sitting in the manager's office, the three of them, the clerk on the edge of his chair. "Why don't you relax a bit and tell it— say, the way you will when you get home tonight."

"If I get home tonight, I shall go straight to bed, sir."

"Too bad," Tully drawled. "Tell us about the woman with the General."

"Well, I'd say she was oh,—I can't judge a woman's age . . . old young or young old!" He fussed with his hands, describing the inadequacy of his speech.

Mrs. Norris leaned forward. "Do you know what a flapper was?"

"Exactly!" the clerk cried. "Thank you very much, madam. And I thought she had a crying jag on at first. In fact she as much as told me she'd been crying. You see, the General upset me terribly with his profanity—just standing there, letting it fall out of his mouth like. I couldn't stand to look at him." The picture made Mrs. Norris and Tully exchange glances. "I gave the precinct officer a verbatim account. You don't want me to go over that again in front of the lady?"

"God forbid," Tully said.

"And the, the flapper—when she got his key, she said: 'He's been sayin' things like that to me all night, so don't you pay him no mind.'" The clerk imitated her drawl.

"Sounds like a southern lady, don't it, Mrs. Norris?" Tully said.

Mrs. Norris nodded, and bit her own lip. It sounded like a voice she herself had heard once or twice before, and once that very morning: "Tell him to please call his broker's office," with the "please" sort of drawn out. "Do you mean to say he wasn't able to walk up and get the key himself?" she asked then.

"Maybe he was able if you say so, madam, but he just stood there leaning on the man and said: "Give the lady the key to my suite you unspeakable—unspeakable—unspeakable."

"Any witness besides yourself?"

"Oh, yes. The telephone operator, Miss Matson. There were guests in the lounge. Our clientele are not the kind to stare. I didn't want to delay him. I gave her the key immediately."

"The man—what would you say he does for a living?" Tully asked.

"Why . . . a salesman, I'd say. Gadgets, maybe to penny arcades. Or maybe juke box records."

"Kind of sharp, huh?"

"Not sharp exactly, but terribly hep."

Tully gave a sniff that wrinkled his nose. "Contemporary of hers or the General's?"

"Closer to her, officer, unless he was tremendously well preserved."

"He'll probably turn out to be a Five Star General himself," the detective said, gathering his legs under him. "I don't suppose anybody called anybody else by name?"

"She called the General: Ransom, I know that, sir."

Mrs. Norris gave a little moan. She could not hold it back.

Tully almost covered it, complaining of age as he got to his feet. "All right, my lad. Let us have the key to Mrs. Norris' room, and we'll give you the green light for home."

"You're very lucky, madam," the clerk said, when they had gone out to where his relief man was on duty and got her the key to 512. "There's only the one room vacant on five."

"It's queer, some people's notion of luck," Tully said, rocking back and forth, his hands in his pockets. "I heard somebody the other day sympathizing with the bad luck of English hangmen. They're going to be out of work soon."

The clerk gave Mrs. Norris' key into the detective's hand, and looked up at him with a truly cherubic face. "I dare say they'll find other employment when they get to know the ropes, sir. Good night."

Tully's face broke into a slow smile. "Bull's-eye," he said. There was nothing in all the world as unpredictable as the human being, he thought.

"Excuse me, young man," Mrs. Norris laid her hand on the clerk's sleeve. "Just one more question. You've been very patient. Was the General carrying anything?"

"I don't think so, madam. But the lady was, I remember it now: a black sort of case, maybe twelve inches long. If I were asked to speculate, I'd say a half dozen steak knives."

Mrs. Norris nodded. "It was the General's medals," she explained, thinking he deserved to know it. "So," she said, as much to herself as to Tully on their way upstairs, "he didn't get them till the last minute."

"Did he keep them in a safe?" Tully ventured.

"They were as often in a pawnshop as they were at home. And I was thinking to myself coming in the car tonight— it would take a particular type of merchant to loan much money on them. Their metal worth can't be more than a few dollars."

"That will bear looking into," Tully said. He put the key in her door, tried to turn it, and discovered the door already unlocked. He was unostentatiously careful, lighting the wall switch, and looking over the room, not wanting to alarm her. Only a forgetful chambermaid, he decided, and put the key in Mrs. Norris' hand. "Goodnight. I hope we meet again soon."

When Mrs. Norris lifted her head to speak to him, a scent of perfume wafted under her nose. She caught the detective's arm and crinkled her nose as she sniffed about the room. Tully then got a whiff of it, too. Without a doubt someone wearing perfume had been in the room not long ago, and they both remembered the operator's remarking that he could smell the scent of the General's companion after she had left the elevator. Questioned now, he could not even smell perfume in the room, much less identify it. Tully could understand that: it was illusive stuff, perfume. Nothing you could put back in the bottle when you'd had enough. Checking with the weary day clerk, he learned that it was not at all possible for the perfume to have belonged to the chambermaid. "In fact," he said, "very vice versa."

Tully regretted having to do it, but he got the girl out of bed to answer the phone. She had been in 512 about eight-thirty, a last check of towels, ashtrays, etc. and she was in the habit of leaving the door open while in a room. She remembered turning off the lights, locking the door, hanging her key ring inside the linen closet door until she went to the maid's room and changed out of uniform, a matter of maybe five minutes' time. Then, as was her custom, she took the key ring downstairs to the desk and went home for the night. She had not heard or seen any activity at 519—almost across the way—to arouse her curiosity.

"Well," the detective said, although nothing in the room indicated the presence of the General's last known companions except the findings of Mrs. Norris' nose, "they were here all the same, I think. And they borrowed her key to lock 519. The General's was inside on the table. Too clever, I'd say, for respectable folk. Looks like they figured on police and reporters cluttering up the halls. They probably just stood in here and waited, could be with the door open a crack. All of which doesn't mean much, except it seems like a lot of precaution to take just because you brought home an old friend drunk. Don't you think?"

Mrs. Norris nodded, her eyes filling with tears of wrath, frustration and sorrow. Tully patted her hand with awkward solicitude. "I don't suppose he ever mentioned her name in your presence?"

"He did not, the old sinner."

15

Mrs. Norris awoke with so violent a start she gave herself a headache, and contrary to her habit, had to lie abed a few moments to get her bearings. It was the second morning out of three she had awakened in an unaccustomed place. But then, these were unaccustomed days. The General was gone, not to some foreign duty—unless a person was romantic about these things. Mrs. Norris was not: dead was dead. And so far as the General was concerned, Mrs. Norris was inclined to be glad fate was that way. He had always had a nasty habit of making his presence felt even when you knew he was five thousand miles away.

High church burial, she supposed. Almost as lenient on its delinquents as Rome, and almost as Popish. Candles likely, his dark suit. She would have to see to that. He had worn it into town . . .

As soon as she put her feet into her slippers she picked up the phone and ordered tea sent up to her and a pot to knock up Master Jamie with as well.

Having refreshed herself with a wash, and the beverage which if it lacked the flavor of tea at least profited by the intention—it was hot—Mrs. Norris called Brooklyn. It was Mr. Robinson who answered the phone, and he was a long time giving her the opportunity to inquire after her sister.

"I was going to call you this very minute, Annie," he started. "The poor old gentleman. Was it a heart attack?"

"Heart failure," she said.

"Uh-huh, uh-huh. It's what we all die of, eh Annie? But him it took sudden. I don't suppose you know yet if he left you anything. Don't misconstrue my meaning now. I wanted to tell you there's a home waiting you here with your sister and me . . ."

That would be the day, thought Mrs. Norris. "Thank . . ."

"Not a word of thanks. It's our natural duty. Was there anyone with the poor old gentleman at the end?"

He could pause long enough when he wanted an answer, she thought, and let the quiet air hang between them until he demanded, "Are you there, Annie?"

"I am. Is Mag there?"

"I thought for a minute we were cut off. The service is not what it used to be, say what you like about mechanical devices. The dial business is not like an operator. Was I rude to you the other night, Annie? It's bothered me since."

"You were not rude to me, Mr. Robinson, but if I was Mag. . . ."

"Ah, I'm glad of that. I have a terrible temper, you know."

"Mr. Robinson, will you stop chattering like a magpie. I have but a minute and I want to speak to my sister."

"Oh, I'm very sorry, Annie. She's out, I think. For a bit of air. She says the only time you can smell the sea is in the early morning, and you know how Mag is for a pure breath of the sea."

"Then I'll call her later in the day, Mr. Robinson."

"Couldn't she call you?"

To say just what he wanted her to say, Mrs. Norris thought. Oh, there was something wrong there all right. "I may not be near a telephone," she said, furious with herself that she could not better cope with him.

"Annie," he purred, and she could hear the smile in his voice, "would you like us to come out and be with you for a day or two? But of course you would. What else is a family for at a time like this? We'll be out tonight now, and not a word, and you won't have to trouble calling Mag today. Is there anything we can bring?"

"Not a thing," she said. "Goodbye, Mr. Robinson."

Beware a man with a glib tongue, she thought to herself, hanging up. What a dislike she had taken to him in the last week, and after a lifetime of toleration. It was the way he had spoken to Mag the other morning that finished it. Coming in at three a.m. with tracks the size of horseshoes under his eyes. And Mag creeping off to bed at one lash of his tongue. Not Annie Norris if he was her man. And now telling her that Mag was out for a sea breeze at eight in the morning. There was no doubt about it—he was not the gentleman she had always thought him.

But then there were not very many gentlemen left in the world. Only one that she could think of at the moment, Master Jamie. She arranged the service of his breakfast.

16

Jimmie stood, teacup in hand, looking down on Fifth Avenue, the green stripe running down its middle through the early traffic. Wherever over the world they were, Irishmen were gathering, and wherever democracy had sanction, the politicians had stayed up the night to help plan the celebration. St. Patrick's Day in the morning.

In the line of such duty, his father had put on his medals before dying. It was like him, and yet bloody unlike him. If he had been alive now he would not have so much as opened the blinds upon the scene. He had always hated daylight before coffee, and Jimmie remembered a remark of his: it was better to see a country only as a terrain map if you had to attack it. When you examined the reverse side of such a nature—the one beneath the shell—it was almost lovable.

Jimmie drained the teacup as the phone rang.

"This is Helene, Jimmie. I am very sorry about your father's death. I hope there is something I can do—that you will let me do."

"Thanks," he said.

"Are you hurt that I left you at the restaurant the other night?"

"Not at the moment," Jimmie said, quite as sharply as his father might have spoken under similar circumstances.

"I guess I deserve that," she said. "Jimmie, there is one thing you must understand for now. More later, but just now—Judge Turner and I were not strangers. I knew his daughter a long time ago."

It must have been a long time ago, Jimmie thought, remembering that he was himself in law school when she went to live in Paris. He could not even remember her name now. "Helene . . ."

"Yes?"

"Later today could you drive Mrs. Norris to Nyack—in father's car—if the police okay it, of course?"

"I'd be pleased to."

"I'll call you in a couple of hours."

"Jimmie. . . . you are very dear to me."

"Thank you, Helene. Thank you very much." He hung up the phone and swallowed down the little lump of rather sad pleasure. Like an adolescent, about once a month he fell in love all over again. Except that in his case it was with the same woman.

Mrs. Norris gave a thump on the door that made him leap for the bathroom. She was soon maneuvering the breakfast cart into the room and setting up the table. At least she had been sensible and was herself having breakfast with him, she and a great tablet and pencil. The efficiency of the women in his life was frightening.

Jasper Tully arrived in time for coffee.

17

"Seems like there was something in what you said, Mrs. Norris," Tully started, "about the General's drinking habits." The preliminary report of the Medical Examiner was in. "One or two drinks was the most he had last night.

Even on an empty stomach, that wouldn't make him dribblin' drunk, would you say?"

Both Jimmie and Mrs. Norris shook their heads.

"What does that leave us with?"

"Him pretending to be drunk?" said Mrs. Norris, and shook her head again. "He was too proud a man for that, Mr. Tully. He wasn't as proud of drinking as he was of holding it."

"Agreed," said Jimmie.

"Which leaves us with the possibility that he was their prisoner and doing a very corny act maybe at gunpoint," Tully said.

"Why?"

"Jimmie, I used to tell you when you were in office, first you got to settle on *what*. Then maybe you have a chance of finding out why."

"What suit was he wearing?" Mrs. Norris asked in the silence that followed Tully's lesson.

"He was wearing the gray tweed when we found him," Jimmie said.

"He wore his dark blue into town," she said.

"He did," Tully confirmed, consulting his notes. "Furthermore, during this trip he wore both suits to the same . . . house. They're both in the laboratory, and both had bits of blond hair. They must know by now whether Angora cat or human."

"I could tell them and I wouldn't need a laboratory for it," Mrs. Norris said with a shrug. "I never knew a cat to run a brokerage."

Mr. Tully cleared his throat.

Poor father, Jimmie thought. "That was a little joke between them, I suppose," he said looking at Tully. "It seems when she called him, she would say it was his broker's office."

"I know," said Tully. "I was talking to people at his club this morning."

"I'd not be surprised if they know more than we do," said Mrs. Norris. "He came home when he felt like behaving, and went to his club when he had notions."

Tully pulled down the corners of his mouth lest they be

caught going up. "You remember the clerk saying she was carrying a box, Mrs. Norris?"

"I do, the box I believe with his medals in it."

"A fair assumption, and we're assuming, too, he put them on before he died. But now here's a curious thing: the medals were all mixed up. I forget what each one is called, but the man I asked knows all about these things, and he says the arrangement was like wearing a Good Conduct medal in precedence over the Congressional Medal of Honor."

"Then she put them on him!" Mrs. Norris cried.

"Dead or alive?" said Jimmie.

Tully nodded. "That's the question, lad. That's it. Maybe the lab will turn up something, but not yet. The Medical Examiner says he died between seven and nine. I think we could be more exact ourselves. But maybe not. The tests are all under way, however. So you can go ahead with plans for the funeral."

Jimmie made his call to Nyack then and there. "The voice of an undertaker," he said, the unhappy business settled, "you can almost hear the organ playing through it while he talks."

"I don't approve of music at funerals," Mrs. Norris said.

"Do you like it at weddings?" said Tully slyly.

"At weddings you don't need it."

True enough, Tully thought, if you looked at it that way. "The Rock's being laid away in old time splendor this afternoon, Jimmie. The boss thought you might like to go. He'd be glad to have you drive out with him."

"Thanks," said Jimmie, not especially keen on spectaculars. But this one, he thought, he had better take in.

"Now," Tully said, "I'd like you to go over the contents of the General's pockets and suitcase with me."

"Will you need me?" said Mrs. Norris hopefully.

"We will," said Tully. "You're quicker witted then the both of us."

The right coat pocket of the General's blue suit had contained two folded pages from the early edition of *The New York Chronicle*, March 16, according to the notation of the police property clerk.

Mrs. Norris needed to overcome a certain reluctance to look at these things which had meant something special to the General. It was like peeping through a keyhole, and with that thought her eyes rested an instant passing over the "Peeping Tom" story to concentrate on the feature of the page as Jasper Tully's bony finger pointed it out—the plans for the St. Patrick's Day parade, including the General's name amongst the very important people to be in the reviewing stand.

The other page, they saw, accounted the pickup order out for Johnny "The Rock" Rocco.

"It seems curious at first, him being interested in that," Tully said, "but down a ways there's your name, Jimmie, and that could be it."

Jimmie nodded and took his father's wallet from the next box. It was something of a shock to look upon the faded picture of his mother, a woman of whom he had no recollection except as her portrait in the living room revealed her. He showed it to Mrs. Norris who sniffed a little. Then he opened the money compartment. He looked twice and then took the money out, each bill separately, and put it on the table, Mrs. Norris giving a small "Oh" at each one hundred dollar bill. Nine of them there were, as well as a fifty and some singles.

"Did you give him all that, Master Jamie?" Mrs. Norris said with deep reprimand.

"I did not. I gave him fifty dollars, two twenties and a ten."

Mrs. Norris pursed her lips. "I wonder what's missing from the house."

Jasper Tully had been watching them. "Did the old gentleman have no money of his own?"

"His pension," Jimmie said, "but it's all tied up in his previous spendings. It will take a better lawyer than I am to straighten out his affairs."

"Well, one thing would look to be clear from it," the investigator said, "If he was murdered it was not for his fortune. Plainly the intention of the pair that brought him home was not to roll him."

"I'd have said that was plain from the beginning," Mrs.

Norris snorted. "Look at her, carrying his medals and calling him Ransom. She knew what was in his pocket and the ways there were of getting it." Mrs. Norris sat down and folded her hands. "Well, the Lord forgive me for saying it, but with all that money in his pocket, the old gentleman must have died happy."

"He lived a good deal happier than most of us, too," Jimmie said. "Let's get on with this business."

But there was nothing else of any value except the parking receipt for his car, a garage on Second Avenue and Sixtieth. The garage stamp indicated that the car had not been moved since Thursday night.

"That's quite a ways from his club," Tully said, "which makes you wonder awful much what it was close to."

"Aye," said Mrs. Norris. "Is that a wealthy neighborhood?"

"Mixed. But no real poverty," Tully said.

"He'd be shy of that, you may be sure."

"Can we have the car now?" said Jimmie.

"I think so," Tully said, picking up the phone. "I'll check and be sure."

Jimmie turned to his housekeeper. "There's someone I've wanted you to meet for a long time, Mrs. Norris, a very dear friend of mine, Helene Joyce. Mrs. Joyce will drive you home—if the car's available."

"How nice," Mrs. Norris said, and brushed vigorously at her dress. It had been her opinion that for a long time he'd been wanting her not to meet Mrs. Joyce. If she didn't watch her Master Jamie it would not be long before the old man's shoes would need resoling. "When do you want me to leave?"

"As soon as you're packed," Jimmie said shortly. He had no patience now with her tantrums.

"Yes, sir," she snapped, and flounced out of the room.

"My God," Jimmie said, when she was gone, "almost a thousand dollars. Where did he get it, Jasp? And in crisp hundred dollar bills."

"There's two possibilities come to mind," Tully said, "a bank—or the horses. All things considered, his Brooklyn jaunt and all that mess, this time, Jimmie, my boy, I'd bet on the horses."

18

As it turned out, Helene was not at all what Mrs. Norris had expected. She looked like a working woman for all her delicate features. Her hand, given with a will on their introduction, had the hardness about it—not roughness but firmness—of competency. Indeed, something inside Mrs. Norris gave a sudden turn, like her soul to the wall. Here was a woman she was going to like in spite of herself, and a woman, she did not doubt, who once she got her foot in the house in Nyack, was likely to bring the other in after it and close the door.

Mr. Tully drove them to the garage. There he identified himself and countersigned the release order. The Jaguar was in plain sight, having been the object of much attention. The technical men had been over it.

"When did the General leave the car?" Tully asked.

"Eight-fifty, sir, Thursday, March fifteenth."

"Were you on duty?"

"Happens, sir, I was."

"Then you know positively it was General Jarvis and not someone else who parked it?"

"Yes, sir. It was the General. Him and I often conversed."

"The car has been here since?"

"Yes, sir.

"Was he in the habit of parking here?"

"At least once a week, sir."

"Overnight?"

"Yes, sir. Sometimes longer. A day or two that is."

"Ever deliver the car to him?" Tully fired these questions, quite unlike his slow-moving self.

"To his club on Thirty-ninth Street."

"Damnation," Tully murmured, slowing down. Then he

was off on another attack. "Did you ever see a lady with him?"

"No, sir, though I thought he had one, if you don't mind me saying so."

"I don't mind if you got a reason," the detective said.

Helene and Mrs. Norris looked at each other.

"He sometimes carried presents or what looked like presents," the attendant went on. "I asked him once if he had grandchildren, meaning in the neighborhood, you see."

"And he said?"

The attendant looked uncomfortably at the women and then plunged on. "He said to me, 'My boy,' he said, 'I have grandchildren on five continents.'"

"And that's how you came to the conclusion he was visiting a lady in the neighborhood?"

"Oh no. Once he had a bottle of perfume. I could smell it."

"Thursday night, did he have any packages?"

"He was in a hurry, sir. I wouldn't say the General was ever frightened, but there was something on his mind. He was quite fidgety."

"Did he have any packages?" Tully hit again. He never asked a question that he did not get an answer to, however much gratuitous information was volunteered him in between.

"Yes, sir, but I can't remember what. I remember him carrying something. . . ."

"Master Jamie's dispatch case!" Mrs. Norris cried. "I remember now him borrowing it in the morning!"

The attendant was nodding his head. "Yes, ma'am, a dispatch case. Like a thin suitcase, and I remember gold initials on it."

"Completely irrelevant," Helene said, "but I gave it to young Mr. Jarvis last Christmas. The initials are J.R.J."

"Better give me a full discription," Tully said.

Helene did, concluding: "And I paid twenty-three dollars for it, plus tax."

"It pays to buy good," Mrs. Norris said, approving just as much Helene's recollection of the exact cost.

Tully gave the boy fifty cents and told him that the ladies

would take the car. "I suppose it could be at his club, the dispatch case," he said then to Mrs. Norris. "Would you have any notions at all as to what was in it?"

She shook her head. "Off and on he's been composing his memoirs. Oh, and I do know he's been rummaging in the attic amongst the family papers for the last week or so. You might just ask Mr. James about it."

Tully nodded and held the door for Mrs. Norris. "Safe home, ladies."

"Where's your shamrock, Mr. Tully?" she asked, looking up in his face.

"Deep in my heart," he said, "where everything is green as spring."

Mrs. Norris gave Helene a poke with her elbow. "Drive on!" she cried, and fastened the veil around her hat.

19

A wallet full of money and a missing dispatch case, Tully thought, as he sat in the car with his notebook in front of him, and the Jaguar's exhaust smoke still in his nose. He tried to blow it out. Roaring little stenches, he thought. They must tell as much of the man who owns them as, say, his handwriting. His own bet of the moment would be that the General's hand was no firmer than smoke, than it had been when he was thirteen years old.

He opened the notebook to a fresh page and began making a timetable from his notes, beginning from where he, of his own knowledge, could begin. He wrote:

Thurs. Mar. 15, 8:15 PM—Water St. Brooklyn.
    "   "   " 8:50 PM—2nd Ave. & 60th, Manh.

He drove then to the General's club, and again was let know they found him a nuisance—because, he thought, in his day the General had been such a nuisance. But this time he saw the people he had missed in his early morning call. He was then able to proceed with his timetable:

Thurs. Mar. 15, 10:40 PM—club, 39th St. near Madison
(clerk put dispatch case in club safe)

Thurs. Mar. 15, 10:45 PM—whiskey at club bar.
(conversa. with Webster Toll who caught 11:13 train for Darien)

About 11 o'clock to card room.

Friday, March 16, 12:45 AM—left call at desk for 9 AM
(can safely presume went to bed)

    9 AM—took call.

    9:05 AM—refused call fr. Broker's office.

    9:30 AM—breakfast in dining room.
(waiter gave him papers, apologized not latest edition.)

    9:50 AM—left club, on foot.

    11 AM—returned to club.
      1. Call to Nyack.
      2. Call to Plaza exchange.
      3. Refused call from broker, but gave message— will call.
      (note order)

    12 noon—took dispatch case from safe.

    12:20 PM—checked in Mulvany.
Needed to wait in lobby few minutes till room ready. Thought to have made phone call.
Requested switchboard not to allow calls through till he said so.

    4:45 PM—call to Eldorado exchange.

    4:50 PM—left hotel with dispatch case, wearing tweed suit.
      (took bath afternoon sometime)

Near the end of a busy day, Tully thought, looking over his record, and just as near the end of a busy life. There was only one big gap in the timetable—from 8:50 when he was at Second Avenue and Sixtieth, and 10:40 when he was at Thirty-ninth and Madison. How did he get from one place to the other? He might have had time to walk, but probably not the inclination. At headquarters, Tully requested a man be put on the cab possibility. He checked with Homicide on what the lab had turned up in the General's car. Nothing, not even the smell of Brooklyn; in fact less than nothing; on the handle, right side, there were no hand or fingerprints at all; clean, wiped clean.

Very, very curious, Tully thought. The General had driven Mrs. Norris in from Nyack Thursday morning, and Tully would give heavy odds that she was a door handle clutcher. Even if she weren't, there had to be some prints on it; the handle of the other door was a smear of them. Someone had deliberately wiped the right one clean.

Which again raised the question of where the General was in Brooklyn. Out of bounds for him at the present, Tully decided, and drove downtown then to see Mr. Webster Toll at his Wall Street office.

20

"It's not that I don't want to cooperate," Mr. Toll said. "I just don't remember. I had been drinking—rather much. My own wife and I had had some differences. Otherwise, I should not have been at the club that late."

Tully nodded his head sympathetically. "'My own wife . . .' That's what you just said, Mr. Toll. That sort of indicates, doesn't it, you and the General might have been talking about . . . his woman?"

Mr. Toll took off his glasses and polished them. "We were talking about women, that's right," he said thoughtfully, "but I suspect in a rather drunken philosophical way . . . you know, their changeability, their ambition for a man. I remember saying that if it weren't for Matilda, I should be well content in a pair of frayed trousers gathering mussels on some small island."

"What did he say to that?"

"I remember that very clearly: 'With or without Matilda?' he said." Toll sat a moment, nodding his head in recollection. "He was telling me that just that evening he had proposed a bit of a trip to his friend. She had refused it; preferred her own apartment with him coming there . . ."

Tully hoped she hadn't changed her mind about a trip. "In fact," Toll went on, "he recommended that I take a mistress. I think 'prescribe' was the word he used. 'Then when something goes wrong you can clear out and no alimony.' And from that I think I got telling him about a friend of mine who is now paying alimony to three ex-wives."

"I don't suppose he called his friend by name, Mr. Toll?"

"I don't suppose he did," the man said. "I don't recall hearing it. They had had a bit of a tiff, I think. He said once or twice that he was not jealous. It was beneath him to be jealous, certainly of a man like that. . . ."

"Like what?" Tully interrupted.

Toll threw up his hands. "You've broken my whole line of thought."

He had known himself it was a mistake the moment he broke in. "It was beneath him to be jealous of a man like that," he prompted.

"Then I said that it was not beneath a man like Othello to be jealous—and he was a pretty fair general. Whereupon, we got into a discussion on whether or not Othello was a good military man, and the psyche of military people. I almost missed my train."

"I guess it's just as well you caught it," Tully said, getting to his feet.

"Oh, indeed it was. Matilda met the last train and that was it."

Tully kept his hat in hand until he passed Toll's secretary on the way out. If he had even seen anyone who looked like a "Matilda" it was she, but then probably all the women in Mr. Toll's life would.

21

A gangster's funeral was always an embarrassment to decent society, but especially to a clergyman. Listening to this one bend all his eloquence toward ambiguity, Jimmie thought it would be a good idea for him on such occasions to recite Mark Antony's "I come to bury Caesar, not to praise him" speech and let it go at that. "The evil that men do lives after them, the good is oft interred with their bones . . ." That turned his thoughts to his father. The old man had known his Shakespeare, and had sometimes lived it. An argument on Othello at the club bar, Tully said. "Beneath him to be jealous of a man like that . . ."

Like whom? The one helping him to play drunk? Someone in Brooklyn? Johnny Rocco? They were contemporaries, by God! And the old man had always liked good whiskey. An acquaintanceship could very well have gone back to Johnny's rum-running days when the General's level of society needed the Johnny Roccos at a party before they could make it a success.

Jimmie shook his head. That line of thought was too horrible to share even with Jasper Tully, and certainly not to be confided to the D.A. Fallon was counting off the limousines lined up outside the funeral chapel. There were three car-loads of flowers.

"I never saw so many Homburg hats," Fallon said, "and look at the cigars lighting up, fifty centers—three for a buck the cheapest."

"We live in prosperous times," Jimmie said. He was watching the license plates of all the great black cars—to small purpose, but he could not help but wonder if Johnny the Rock had not had his last ride-but-one in one of them. "It's a *Who's Who* of the underworld, isn't it?"

"And every goddamned man of them has accounted his whereabouts while Johnny went bye-bye," the D.A. said.

"Now that's remarkable in itself," said Jimmie, "don't you think?"

The D.A. grunted. "You should hear some of the alibis. Nick Casey was trying to get out of a Peeping Tom nab in night court."

"Did he make it?"

"Only when he got his girl friend in for corroboration. His defense was very funny. You should hear old Henny tell it: 'For Chrissake, Judge, what'd I want lookin' in a window at some dame in her bare feet? I got a whole row of 'em on my payroll, and they don't wear nothin' but a piece of string!' "

The last limousine pulled out into the cortege, white with purple trim. "Sic transit Rocco," Jimmie said.

"Born Giuseppe," the D.A. said. "Well, that's one way to get deported." He looked at his watch. "Want to take a look at that joint on Water Street?"

"Very much," said Jimmie, but wishing fervently that it was not one of the last places his own father had been seen alive.

It was mid-afternoon when they drove up to Minnie's Diner. In the daytime Minnie had the appearance of being legitimate. There was at least a stack of dirty dishes in the sink which the restaurant keeper was tackling himself. There were, however, three telephones in the place—a fact so obviously suspicious that Jimmie thought most investigators would discount it.

Fallon ordered coffee and made no secret of his identity. "How come the three phones, Minnie?"

"One for me, one for my customers . . . and one for you. You want to make a phone call?"

"Pretty cool," the D.A. said, the sides of his mouth down.

"You got jurisdiction in Brooklyn?" Minnie asked, and Jimmie thought he'd been put through the works in the past couple of days.

"I've got friends here," Fallon said.

"Me, too. In a pig's eye."

"Was Johnny Rocco a friend?"

"If he was, I'd be at the funeral," Minnie said.

"We were looking for you, a real slam-bang affair."

"I'll read about it in the paper."

They were getting nowhere and not very fast either, Jimmie thought, and when he got the chance, he asked the man how long he'd been in business here.

"Since my wife died," he said. "That's going on two years. It was her place, see, but I decided to try and make a go of it. A man's got to make a living."

"And what did you do before your wife died?"

"Five years at Sing Sing, and you know it as well as I do, damn your souls! Now get the hell out of here and come back with warrants if you want in. The one thing I learned up the river, my rights!"

It was not very easy to leave Minnie's with dignity after that, but to make a show of it, Jimmie stood at the curb, his topcoat open, his hands in his pants' pockets. He scanned the neighborhood: The Tower Foundry and Iron works, Schwartz's steel bearings, Robinson's Printing . . .

"Let's go," Fallon said. "We're not going to get anything out of that baby."

"Right," Jimmie said. "But mark my words, Fallon, that boy is clean. An ex-con who wasn't could not afford the luxury of kicking a D.A. out of his place."

"Minnie can't afford it either," Fallon said grimly.

Jimmie thought that attitude a great mistake on the part of Fallon. It was the enemy of an open mind. On the whole, it was a good thing for the District Attorney that he had a man like Jasper Tully. But then what D.A. would be worthy of his office if part of him wasn't a Jasper Tully, Jimmie decided, remembering how often the investigator had made him look good.

22

"There are messages coming from all over the world," Mrs. Norris greeted Jimmie when he reached Nyack toward evening. "And a basketful from Washington. Mrs. Joyce has been answering the phone all afternoon."

"I suppose there'll be people tonight," Jimmie said.

"By the tens and hundreds. Would you like a drink in your room while you dress?"

"Couldn't we all take time for one in the living room?"

"Your father's been laid out there."

"Oh," said Jimmie, "of course. I'll have it upstairs." The smell of flowers permeated the house. It was heathenish, Jimmie thought. He beat his retreat upstairs as soon as he could. Mrs. Norris had managed to rub a bit of Presbyterianism off on him.

"She's a plainer woman than I thought," the housekeeper said, bumping the door closed behind her when she brought the whiskey and ice.

"If you mean Mrs. Joyce, I think she's beautiful."

"I mean there's no fancy trimmings about her. She speaks her mind and thinks straight."

"Oh," said Jimmie. "That she does."

Mrs. Norris stood on one foot and then the other. She was not waiting to be offered a drink, Jimmie thought, having brought but one glass. Finally he asked: "Is something troubling you?"

"No, of course not. You'll have your dinner buffet off the kitchen. Mr. Jamie . . . how will you introduce her to people tonight?"

"Helene? Why, as Mrs. Joyce. How else?"

"You couldn't say . . . 'my fiancée'?"

"My God," said Jimmie, "You have been impressed! Or is it respectability you're worried about?"

Mrs. Norris folded her arms. "If I was worried about respectability, I'd have been out of this house a long time before now." She turned on her heel and stomped to the door.

Jimmie called to her: "Mr. Tully will be here soon. He'll be spending the night."

"And my sister and brother-in-law are coming. Where will I put Mr. Tully?"

"In father's quarters. That's how he wants it."

Jimmie wondered, dressing, if there had been any discussion between Helene and Mrs. Norris to warrant such a suggestion. He drained his glass and paused on his way downstairs to see which room she had put Helene in. It would tell better than words Mrs. Norris' estimation of the woman. It could not have been higher. The light shone from beneath the door of the north bedroom, and if he was not mistaken, it was from there that the smell of wood smoke was coming: the housekeeper had lighted the fire in the grate. Jimmie tapped on the door.

"Come!"

He opened the door a bit and stuck his head in. "Are you decent?"

"If clothes will do it, enormously. Come by the fire—or the window. I'm torn between them."

"I'm not," said Jimmie, taking her in his arms and holding her close. The kiss was long and soft with but the faintest stirring of passion at its end, so that Helene withdrew and took his hand to lead him to the window.

"It's changed," she said, speaking of the river with the sky's color on it, "from when last I looked."

Jimmie looked at her only. "'How many loved your moments of glad grace . . . The sorrows of your changing face.' Damn. I've forgot a whole patch of that."

Helene smiled and squeezed his hand. "The people's candidate. You are an egghead, Jimmie. What will they do to you?"

"I don't even know what I want them to do to me. It all seems so long ago, that afternoon in Albany. I wanted very much to be governor then. Now I want the leisure to live a little, quietly, and hear wood fires crackling and remember full poems and not snatches of them. And I want terribly to make love to you."

"We are both so vulnerable to each other now, darling."

"Does love hurt you that much, Helene?"

"I have been looking at the face of someone out there. I loved a boy and lost him, and a man loves me whom I respect and whom I yield . . . Jimmie, there is something I must tell you about Madeline Barker and the Judge."

"You have no idea," he said with all the cold hurt he could manifest, "how much jollier I'll find that story with a drink in my hand. I'll be in the kitchen with Mrs. Norris. When your boy out there disappears, you might like to join us."

Helene lifted her chin and did not move or speak until he was gone. Jimmie could not have felt more miserable; he had thought this sort of thing was over between them, the raising of ghosts whenever he neared the subject of matrimony.

Mrs. Norris took one look at him and got a tray of ice cubes from the refrigerator. "Aw, lad," she said, "you've no sense of tactics at all."

"What the devil do you know about it?" Jimmie cried.

The gardener who, on necessary occasions, doubled as houseman, wandered in then to say there were callers paying their respects in the living room. When Jimmie returned to the kitchen, Mr. Tully had arrived and was warming his hands at the grate. Helene was slicing bread.

"The course of true love never does run smooth," the investigator was saying over his shoulder, and unaware of Jimmie's presence.

"To say nothing of the course of false love," Jimmie said.

Tully screwed his ugly head around and squinted at him. "What, my boy, is false love—is there such a thing?"

Jimmie was hooked on his own hasty cast. "Love of self," he said, somewhat steadying his position.

"Oh, that runs smooth as butter," Tully said. "The trouble is it never gets a man anywhere. Now as I was about to say, it seems the General and his fair lady had a tiff after he rushed home to her from Brooklyn. He couldn't have got

there before nine, and at ten-twenty-five he was on Third
Avenue and Fifty-first Street where he caught a cab down to
his club."

Jimmie repeated the address, and that of the parking lot—
Sixtieth and Second. "There's a lot of city in there, Jasp."

Tully nodded. "One side or the other, he did a bit of
walking. Then when he got to his club he complained at the
bar to a gentleman named Webster Toll, that his fair lady
had refused to go on a trip with him."

Jimmie and Mrs. Norris exchanged glances. No word of
the proposed trip had ever come to them, but it might have
been the reason for all the cash, whatever its source.

Helene put the bread in a basket and suggested they eat
something before more people arrived. Tully finished his
account at the buffet: "The General wound up saying he
was not jealous, that it was beneath him to be jealous,
certainly of a man like that. Now who would you say he was
talking about?"

Jimmie shook his head. "It could have been anyone from
the Secretary of State to . . ."

"To Johnny Rocco?" Tully prompted. Then he went on
to outline his own speculations about the old Johnny Rocco,
whose career he had checked up on that afternoon. The
Rock had been a very dapper fellow in the twenties, and
more than one gentleman of means had invited him to his
party—providing he brought enough whiskey, of course.

Jimmie, having made exactly the same speculation, had
to admit the possibility of such an association. He himself
had not been old enough to remember, however.

"You forget," said Mrs. Norris, "I was around then, too,
and of an age to remember, and I can tell you there was no
man by that name ever in your father's house. The first time
I ever heard of this Rocco person was when you, Master
Jamie, were District Attorney."

"Well," Tully said, "that cancels out another afternoon's
work." He looked around the table, the buffet . . .
"What kind of a family is this, a wake without a drop of
whiskey?"

"Oh," said Mrs. Norris, "I was getting the ice when you
came."

"Never mind the ice," said Tully with a wink at Helene, "it's already broken." He lifted his glass when they all had one: "To the old gentleman, God rest him. Whatever else he's done to it, he's certainly brought some new light into my life."

"I think I can say the same," said Mrs. Norris, and God knows it was true, she thought. It was only Thursday on her way to Brooklyn that she was contemplating how little exciting ever happened to her nowadays. And right now she could truly say she had not felt better in many a long year. But thinking of Brooklyn she was reminded of the Robinsons. Poor Mag . . . Strange, until Thursday, if she admitted the truth now, since almost the day she met him, she would have said, "Poor Mr. Robinson."

Helene and Jimmie drank and ate without comment.

23

"I remember him when . . ."

"Do you remember the day he . . ."

"Let me tell you about when he came back from . . ."

Such were the whispered commencements to conversations all over the house. A military guard had taken up the watch, and the living room, the library, the hall, the stairs were crowded with people remembering the General and the various milestones of his busy life. It was great tribute to the old man, Jimmie thought, that there was more subdued laughter than letting of tears.

He was on the stairs himself, his arm in the clasp of an ex-envoy to Sweden, when what he called "the political contingent" arrived. He had expected Judge and Mrs. Turner, but for them to come in the company of Big Mike Zabriski and Miss Barker seemed poor taste to Jimmie. But then taste was an uncommon word in politics. Jimmie found for the diplomat a contemporary with whom to share reminiscences, and went down to Mrs. Turner who opened her arms to him and gave his cheek a tearful kiss.

Jimmie took the hand Madeline Baker offered him. But in the middle of her sympathetic gaze her eyes caromed off his check and fastened on someone behind him. She excused herself and as he turned, he saw her make a mercurial journey to Helene.

Mrs. Turner was watching also. "So she's here, too," she said.

"Mrs. Joyce is a dear friend," Jimmie said.

The Judge was solicitous of his wife. "Madeline will manage, my dear," he murmured; and practically in the same breath so that Jimmie had no opportunity to speak his annoyance, the Judge went on: "Touching story in the afternoon papers, Jimmie, about your father's managing his medals before dying. Very like him, don't you think?"

"Rather," Jimmie said.

"That was Madeline's release, by the way."

By the way . . . Jimmie thought. The Judge was trying hard to ingratiate Madeline with him of late. Then it occurred to him: what the devil was Madeline doing, giving a release to the papers about General Jarvis' death? James Jarvis did not belong to his party body and soul, family and fortune.

"Yes, just like the man I best remember—duty first, death second," the Judge went on.

Jimmie tried hard not to be harsh on him. Many a wise man spouted gibberish in the presence of a corpse which by some little chance of fate was not his own. Jimmie excused himself, laid his hand a moment on Big Mike's shoulder, passing, so that he would not need to pause there for more such morbid sentiment.

Mike's contribution echoed after him: "Well, it comes to all of us. The older the better, I say."

"You didn't know your Mrs. Joyce and I once were intimates, did you, Jimmie?" Madeline smiled as he joined them.

"I may have heard it and forgotten," Jimmie said coldly. He was wondering at the moment if ever she had written anything on a subway wall.

"You haven't really changed, Helene. Only I have changed," Madeline mourned.

"It is hard to discern it with chameleons," Helene said. "And long ago I ceased to care. Only you and the Turners cherish painful recollections. Poor Jimmie, he knows nothing of what we're saying."

Madeline threw back her head as though to laugh, but remembered in time the occasion of this meeting. "You mean to say you haven't told him of our Bohemian days?"

Jimmie was distinctly uncomfortable. It was like two women undressing before him; one at a time would be interesting, but two was nihilistic.

"I don't cherish mine with that much affection," Helene said. "I lost something very dear to me."

"So did the Turners," Madeline snapped.

"But look what they gained in you, my dear. To lose a daughter and gain another?"

"For God's sake put away your arrows," Jimmie said.

Helene laid her hand on his arm. "No, Jimmie. Let's count them now, but not in front of all these people. Couldn't we go into your study?"

Jimmie did not like to take them there. It was a place he wished to keep inviolate. But he had little choice. Nor was he placated much when both women paused in their baiting of each other to compliment him on it. He lit cigarettes for them and filled a pipe for himself. "I can't stay long," he murmured.

Helene smiled. "Like they say, that's the story of my life." She lifted her head: "Very well, I shall be both brief and blunt. When I was an artist's model—more years ago than I care to number—I had a friend who ran away from her high-born kinsmen, from a house that was as cold as her father's justice. Her name was Margaret Turner. And she had a college friend named Madeline who doesn't belong in the story yet except for a chance introduction. Margaret and I shared everything—including my assignments as an artist's model. After a while I was married . . . common-law we called it, but in my mind it was binding. How ironic it is, when I think of it now, that I am the one accused!"

Helene got up and started to pace back and forth.

Madeline watched her rather as though she thought she might plunge for escape. Jimmie pulled at his pipe.

"Perhaps you can guess the rest, Jimmie? I was faithful to the faithless. I lost the husband to my friend, and both of them to Paris, where as the story goes, they are living happily ever after." She whirled around on the other woman. "Now comes Madeline, a veritable Joan of Arc. Perhaps you'll account your contribution?"

"It's very simple," Miss Barker said, "I was the one who told."

"Not that simple, it isn't," Helene said. "She came searching for her friend to me, and soon pretended herself my friend, and got the story from me. The Judge paid you, didn't he?"

"Many times over," Miss Barker said, and there was something in her way of saying it that touched Jimmie as nothing she had ever said in his presence had.

"The trouble was she did not use the word 'wife' in my instant, when she told the story to His Honor. I was all blame—and I had no papers, no wedding words to prove my honor. In other words, Jimmie, I took the rap for corrupting the Judge's daughter. In time he got a copy of a French wedding certificate to look at, the bona fide Mrs. Gregory Joyce. But she would not come home to her parents' house. And Madeline would not leave it. She had bought herself a home at the expense of my reputation."

"Now things have greatly changed," Miss Barker said. "Your reputation could buy you almost anything."

Jimmie swore a violent oath beneath his breath.

But Helene shrugged. "That does not even anger me any more, but now you know why Judge Turner sent you home to bed, Jimmie. I am not good company. In fact, I am still unclean in spite of the fact that he took me home with him that night and tried to fumigate me. How does the song go—'wash me in the water that you washed your dirty daughter?' . . ."

"I don't get it," Jimmie said.

"'. . . And I will be as pure as the whitewash on the wall.' Now do you get it?"

"No!"

"He asked me if I would like a fellowship to work in England. He has much admired my work, you see," she said with mock naiveté, "after all these years, and out of the work of all the sculptors in America, mine deserved a fellowship . . . created overnight."

"It was a legitimate offer, Helene, and not created overnight," Madeline said quietly. "The endowment relates to a small estate outside London. I once administered it."

Jimmie got a start then that made him glad the women were attending only each other at the moment. His first personal encounter with Madeline Barker had related to England after the Albany meeting. Jimmie looked at the women who was calmly watching Helene move about like a restless panther. Very sure of herself, Madeline Barker, much in control. He got to his feet and caught Helene's hand in his, drawing her to some ease at his side. The hand was cold and damp, and he was reminded of the feeling when someone has long dangled her fingers in the water from a boat. He lifted it to his lips, the public display of affection costing him considerable discomfiture.

Madeline looking from him to Helene smiled a little and dropped her eyes as though deeply hurt. That really embarrassed him. She looked up again immediately and fiercely. The softness had been but a moment's lapse. "Mrs. *Joyce*," she said, and her voice sounded choked up, "what touching loyalty to a lost cause, your having kept that name for all these years." She got to her feet. "That makes you almost as pitiable as me. I'll be forty-five soon, Helene, an acknowledged spinster." She looked a moment at the doorknob before putting her hand to it. "In that regard, I do believe the only difference between us is the light in which we have conducted our affairs. Goodnight, all."

"Now there," said Jimmie as the door closed on her, "is a witch if ever I saw a broom."

"No," Helene said, slowly, "I do believe the years have touched her with humanity. I think she is in love with you."

As long as he lived, Jimmie thought, he would never understand the perceptivity of women.

"No more scenes like that, Jimmie," Helene said smiling up at him, "you might learn to reciprocate."

"Just what do you mean by that?"

"Public confession."

"Heaven forbid!" said Jimmie.

24

Mrs. Norris hung up the phone and sat down heavily. The Robinsons were not coming. Mag was not feeling very well. "I've put her to bed, Annie. No more than her stomach, I think. She'll be fine in the morning."

Oh, a very cheerful man was Mr. Robinson. But the fact remained, she had not seen her sister, nor heard her voice, since the morning at three when Mr. Robinson came home and ordered Mag to bed when she questioned where he had been all night.

But why had he said they were coming if he had no such intention? And the answer to that was plain enough: when she expected to see Mag that night in Nyack, she was sure not to try to see her in Brooklyn before it. And once in Nyack, what with the house in mourning, callers streaming in from over the country, politicians poking under the carpets, and the funeral still ahead of them, Mrs. Norris was not likely to interfere with Mr. Robinson's ministrations to his wife.

And then of course it could all be her imagination, considering the things going on in this house.

Mrs. Norris jumped when Tully spoke to her. "I thought you were out of the way for the night," she said.

"I wondered if you could use any iodine," the investigator drawled.

"If I could use any or if I have any?"

"If you could use some. The old gentleman had three bottles of it, and by the looks of it, all bought at Shea's Drug Store recently. You don't think he had in mind trying suicide?"

"No more than I would," she said, and thought about it further.

Tully shook his head. "What on earth would a man buy three bottles for?"

Mrs. Norris shrugged. It was too much for her mind in its present condition.

"There's something else I've been wanting to go over with you," Tully said, "if you're not too tired."

She made up her mind then to concentrate on what he was saying. "Go ahead, Mr. Tully."

"When the General arrived at his hotel last night with his fair lady and the other one, do you remember what he said to the clerk?"

"Something profane, wasn't it?"

"But besides that. I got the exact transcript from the precinct man. 'Give the lady the key to my suite, you so-and-so, etcetera.' Now the General didn't have a suite. He had a room. And if I'm not mistaken, he was the kind of man to call a room a room, eh?"

Mrs. Norris nodded.

"But his fair lady, now, that's something else. Her notion of where the likes of the General ought to be staying, and her notion of the Mulvany, would put the word 'suite' in her mouth."

Mrs. Norris leaned forward. It was easy enough now to concentrate. "You have the ingredients of something there, Mr. Tully."

"Thank you, Mrs. Norris. The trouble is, I don't know what it's going to cook up into."

She put one finger on Mr. Tully's hand where it was resting on the telephone. "Was he hypnotized, do you think?"

"That's the line of inquiry I'm about to pursue. The troublesome thing about it—he was a man of such strong will."

"He was strong enough willed, as you say, Mr. Tully, but there were times he didn't have much won't."

Mr. Tully put in a call to New York to a psychiatrist of his acquaintance. It was possible for the General to have been hypnotized and set in a drunken pattern—except that, having never been slobbering drunk himself, he would probably over-act.

"He'd probably over-act," Tully repeated for Mrs. Norris' benefit. And that was certainly what he had done. The detective then asked his friend about the probabilities in the arrangement of the medals. When he hung up he repeated the gist of the opinion to Mrs. Norris. "If he put them on himself in the state of hypnosis, thinking himself drunk, he might've deliberately mixed 'em up."

"That doesn't help much as I see it," Mrs. Norris said.

"Nope, we're never going to get three multiplying one by two," Tully said, and started upstairs again. "Think about that iodine," he added, pausing, "was he accident-prone, as they say?"

"He was very steady, Mr. Tully, the nerves of an aristocrat." When he was gone, Mrs. Norris picked up the phone herself and called Shea's Drug Store, inquiring when the General had bought the iodine. No one knew, and checking the Jarvis account the clerk discovered that the purchase had not been charged, although the old gentleman was in the habit of charging everything.

"Indeed he was," Mrs. Norris said to herself, taking the information up to the detective. "He never paid for a thing he could get on tick."

"More of his aristocratic ways," Tully said. "But it's on the label: Shea's Drug Store. You're a perceptive woman, Mrs. Norris. Thank you for the information." He entered a note in his book. He then pointed to the portrait without raising his head. "Who's that?"

"That, Mr. Tully, was once the President of the United States."

"I thought he was familiar," Tully said. "You must excuse my ignorance, Mrs. Norris, but I'm a long time out of school, and I'll tell you the truth, I don't think I've heard of him since."

"He was a distant relative."

"He looks it," Tully said, "I've been going over the old gentleman's memoirs. I have to do that, you know, looking for clues."

"They're not in my keeping."

"I'm sure they're not, from what I've read," Tully said. "He has snatches of all sorts of tales written out on separate pages—as though he thought to patch them together like a puzzle. It would make quite a book, you know, though by his notations there were things about people he didn't dare publish."

"Were there?" she said. "I wonder, Mr. Tully, I often ask myself, did some of the things he talked about really happen, or did he make them up? He had a lively imagination."

"He did that," said Tully, "whether or not he made them up."

"He used to come down to the kitchen and purposely rile me, to see how much I would take of his mischief. Do you know, Mr. Tully, I got so that I wouldn't even blush? And that made him furious. He'd ask me if I had no modesty— me, mind you, and stomp up the stairs like a bull . . ." That turned her mind to something else. "Did you ask Master Jamie about the family papers?"

Tully nodded. "All he knows is that the General was thinking of bringing out an edition of the President's letters. I've put out an inquiry of all the major publishers— including the one which contracted for his memoirs. None of them gave him a thousand dollars."

"That's what I was wondering," Mrs. Norris said.

"But I'm still waiting for his agent to call me back. Seems like he got a sudden urge to go fishing. I wouldn't think so much of that except he had to buy a rod, a reel, boots . . . the works. His wife says it's the first time he ever went in his life. Now that isn't a disease that comes on a man sudden, Mrs. Norris. Well, we'll see in a day or two. Maybe he'll come back for the funeral. Keep your eyes open there, Mrs. Norris. Look out through your tears and see who else is watering the old fellow's grave."

"I will. I hope you'll be comfortable for the night."

"I will if the ghosts'll let me," he said with a wink.

25

By evening of the next day, Sunday, Tully had learned very little more of General Jarvis' intimate life than he knew when he came, of his recent intimate life, that was. The study was strewn with accounts of "the old days," but the detective could find no reference to anyone who answered the description of the woman who had brought him home to the Mulvany. No surprises at all, Tully thought unhappily, unless it was in the General's handwriting: the detective had been wrong about that thinking it probably childish. The old man had written an elegant hand, neat and controlled. Tully had consulted an expert on hypnotism. For the present he could see no purpose to consulting the hand-writing experts. They were not a lot to inspire confidence anyway. A carnival sort mostly.

The detective was sitting in the study chair opposite the President's portrait at that moment. A queer feeling came over him. He had been joking about the ghosts the night before. He was by no means a superstitious man, but at the instant it was like fifty years being snatched from his own life: he could have sworn he heard someone saying, "You're getting warm."

Why the devil should he think of a childhood game . . . here? Probably in this room as a child the General himself had visited his own father, and got advice he didn't take. Except for the General, there were two hundred years' of lawyers in the family, including this old geezer on the wall. "Excuse me, Mr. President," Tully muttered, half-jest, half-earnest.

A person got a funny feeling sitting under his stare, the heavy-lidded eyes. He was a character, too, no doubt. Tully tried to put himself back in the mental state where he had felt "warm." How was it the hotel clerk had described the

General's male companion? Salesman, maybe of gadgets for a penny arcade. And the elevator boy: circus maybe, fight promotor . . . that carnival spirit . . . carnival . . .

There was a knock at the door and Tully's reverie was over. Jimmie came in and introduced the man with him, August Fowler, the General's literary agent.

Fowler shook hands perfunctorily and then made quite a business of staring up at the picture. "So that's him. I remember seeing the picture in my seventh grade history. American History, seventh grade. Or was it eighth? Interesting looking face, don't you think?"

Since the question was asked of no one in particular, no one answered him. Jimmie told the investigator: "It seems father came on a diary of the President—not as dull as we had thought his life might have been. Fowler, here, agreed to submit it for publication."

"You know, Jarvis, it would be a fine idea for you to go ahead with what your father planned—write an introduction. Good for you too."

"In what way?" said Jimmie.

"Is it a secret you plan to run for governor? It was no secret to your father certainly. He told me about it."

Tully had been watching him while he talked. A sharp forty-five, he decided, a press agent who had taken a post-graduate course and got himself a literary license. "When did all this happen, Mr. Fowler?"

Fowler jerked his head around, as though the cat had spoken to the king. "Oh, yes. I'd forgotten. You are the police."

"*A* police," Tully amended. "When was it you last saw the General?"

"May I take it from the beginning of the diary episode?"

"Why not?" Tully drawled. "Take it from a chair, too, if you like." He gestured the man into one of the General's easy chairs. Jimmie half sat on the desk.

"On Thursday night he called me at home," Fowler started.

"What time?"

"After nine. We had dinner guests and were just leaving the table. I suppose you'd like to know where he called from?"

Jimmie merely raised his eyes and Tully drawled: "What makes you think so, Mr. Fowler?"

The agent looked from face to face and then leaned back. "Why, before the General came into my office the next morning—on an appointment we had made over the phone—I had a call for him. It was from . . . his broker's office. And I think we are agreed, gentlemen, that General Jarvis did not have a broker?"

Tully noticed the little muscles of anger working at Jimmie's mouth. This guy was too familiar, too smooth, too much the son of a bitch. "I'm not sure I'd agree to that," Tully said, "Would you, Jimmie?"

"Not at the moment, I won't," said Jimmie.

"I beg your pardon," Fowler said. "Let's put it this way then: *I* don't believe he had a broker. Not with a southern accent asking for 'Ransom' on the phone."

That was a score and no doubt of it, Tully thought. "As a matter of fact, we would like to know just where the General was Thursday night, Fowler."

"Now, I'm in a funny spot," the agent said. "Actually, I don't know. I thought I had the phone number, but I couldn't find it today when I looked for it. You see when he called me, I asked to call him back and jotted down the number. I do know it's an Eldorado exchange."

Tully nodded. More confirmation. That was all. But he made a note. The General had called EL at a quarter of five from his hotel room. Now at least they could place exact limits on the area where the fair lady dwelt: within the Eldorado Exchange.

"Now," Fowler went on, "since she called my office Friday morning, I can only assume he gave her the number or else jotted it down on a pad at her house. A fair assumption, Mr. Tully?"

"Reasonable anyway," Tully said.

"Thank you," the agent said with sarcasm. "Now I shall volunteer an impression for what it's worth to you. When he called, I suspected he was trying to impress somebody. Frankly, I pegged it an amatory tactic. When his broker called, I was sure that's what it had been, and I was not in very great hopes of getting anything special in the way of a manuscript."

"And did you get something special?"

"I wouldn't say so," the agent pursed his lips. "Still, it's not dull . . . as some of these things are. I was pleasantly surprised."

"You really feel you can get it published?" Jimmie said.

"As I told your father, I should like to try. There are what is known as prestige books. As a matter of fact, I should like to proceed. With your permission. No hurry of course, I don't suppose another hundred years would make much difference."

Hurry up and stand still, Tully thought. "Did you bring it with you, the diary?"

"No. It's in my office safe."

Suddenly mighty precious, Tully thought, for something that laid in an old trunk for a hundred years. "Just what are the royalties on a thing like this liable to come to?"

"Possibly no more than a thousand dollars advance," Fowler said. "If they caught on—they have a sort of archaic splendor, you might say,—they might make all of us a bit of money."

"Poor father," Jimmie said, thinking how long ago the old boy would have dug out the diary had he but known a scratch of its worth. "Did he press you for money, Fowler?"

Fowler made a deprecating gesture. "I wouldn't say that. I knew him well enough to be circumspect in my promises."

"Did he get any?" Tully asked bluntly.

"I am not in the habit of paying money before it's in the house," Fowler said. "I can't afford it."

That was not an answer, not absolutely, Tully thought. But he would wait a while and get at it another way. "When did he bring the book to you?"

"First was the ten o'clock appointment. He was at my office on schedule. We merely talked. I suppose you might call it a briefing. He spoke to me from a few notes he had written out. Quite eloquently. I said if he could make the introduction and commentary as good, and if the diary had the merit he thought, I would try to place it. He said then that he would bring it in that afternoon. And that is exactly what he did. At five o'clock, he brought the diary to my office. I saw him but a moment, as my secretary will testify."

"Why should your secretary need to testify?" Tully said, leaning forward in the General's chair.

"Wasn't General Jarvis murdered?"

"Not that we've been able to prove so far. But any such information you can give us would get full consideration."

"Oh, no. I've given you what I know." He seemed to be genuinely shocked.

"Was that why you went fishing, yesterday—thinking the General was murdered?" Tully asked.

"Certainly not. I had promised a friend a week ago. I was already in North Carolina when I heard that General Jarvis was dead."

"Didn't you read the paper yesterday morning?"

"I didn't have time. Nor the desire. When I take a vacation, it's complete."

"Anybody we know—your friend?" Tully said easily.

"I doubt it."

"Try us."

Fowler looked at him venomously. Plainly the agent liked him as little as the detective liked the agent. "Wilson Dram, the writer," he said.

"I've been wanting to go fishing a long time myself," Tully said, "I understand from Mrs. Fowler you got yourself some new equipment. Get a good buy?"

"Not very."

"Where? so I'll be sure not to go there."

"King's Mart on Forty-third Street."

Tully nodded. "I'll remember. I don't suppose the General left his dispatch case in your office?"

"No. But I remember him carrying it. Yours wasn't it, Mr. Jarvis? I remember the initials, JRJ."

"It's mine, wherever it is," Jimmie said.

"I'm glad to have met you, Mr. Fowler," Tully said, getting up from the General's desk.

Fowler left without shaking hands. After he had seen him

to the front door, Jimmie came up again. "What do you think, Jasp?"

Tully was making notes. "I'd like to have heard his story if he didn't think the General was murdered. Still, it's just about as hard, Jimmie, for him to sort out the lies he's going to tell as it is for us to sort 'em out after he's told them. That's what I'm working at now, by the way."

26

The General's funeral was a magnificent pageant. It became an ancient warrior, some tribal chieftain, Jimmie thought, whose progeny would divide the kingdom and then war upon each other. And there, perhaps because the sermon was so dull in contrast to the setting, Jimmie thought for the first time of a will. The old man might not have had anything to leave, but he might at least have registered his good intentions. And it might carry the name of his mistress. But surely Jasper Tully had thought of that. . . .

The General's funeral was an insult to civilized man. Pomp and circumstance. There were flowers here by the bushel, there was a wreath you'd expect to see around the neck of a horse after he won the Kentucky Derby, Mrs. Norris thought. But at the cemetery when taps sounded, she dabbed her eyes, and for the first time remembered Mr. Tully's advice: watch who else is watering the grave. Matrons, they were for the most part, the women of old families, who wore their money as easy as a good pair of gloves. Unostentatious wealth: the minks between them and the damp winds looked as natural as squirrels to the woods. And there wasn't a car of violent hue in all the mile's caravan of them. Glimpsing the cars nearest, from under her veil, Mrs. Norris saw a face in the window of a black limousine. She groped for the hand of Helene who was standing next to her, for her own heart had begun to thump.

She gave Helene's hand a fierce squeeze, and pulled her close.

"Look at the woman's face in the car with the man at the wheel," she whispered. All the other chauffeurs were standing together.

In the time it took Helene to locate the car, the man had started its motor.

"They're going. Quick!" Mrs. Norris said.

But she was asking the impossible of Helene or herself at a graveside. Neither of them could very well pick up her skirt and run. Helene, however, was graceful enough to move without plunging, and quick enough to see the face of the driver: round as a moon with but a night or two's wane, and the color of yellow wax, like a faded sunburn. She could not see the woman at all. But she got the license number.

Mrs. Norris lingered at the grave long enough to ask one of the attendants if there was a card on the large gaudy wreath. There was none, but he remembered the man delivering it; brought it right to the cemetery, a fellow in a black chauffeur's suit that didn't fit him. Looked like he was going to burst it. In fact, he looked like he was going to burst his skin, a moon of a face . . .

When they got back to the house, Mrs. Norris called Mr. Tully at the New York District Attorney's office, and told him. She also gave him the license number Helene had taken, and promised to come into the city herself the next afternoon.

27

Jasper Tully had thought of the will. It was one of the things he had expected to see, spending Saturday night and Sunday in the country, and since he had been given carte blanche in the General's rooms, he had searched it out among the old gentleman's papers. A very simple affair it was: leaving both his assets and his debits to his only legitimate son, James Ransom Jarvis. It had been drawn up in 1945, and interestingly, initialed and dated in the presence of a notary once a year since. It was a blister of notary stamps. And the obvious intention was to show it as the one and only testament of Ransom Jarvis.

Just one more item of interest in the legend of the General. Tully was rapidly filling his notebook with them. At this rate he could soon write the old rake's biography himself.

Meanwhile the detective had undertaken to do his own leg work, from broker's to broker's—the pawn brokers' shops of Eighth Avenue. Many a rookie cop walked this beat. He had pounded its like himself—too long ago. Here was the dividing line between respectability and the downbeats. A woman fed the pigeons—clouds of them—from a paper bag, the two-bit con men spotted tourists and gave them the damnedest welcome to New York City, Buddy, can you spare five bucks? The jukeboxes moaned the whole day long; old time vaudevillians met as though by chance and regaled each other with the same old tales of going on the road so long ago the dust rose from the wagon wheels; actors sped to rehearsal, last night's rolled drunks to pawn five-dollar cuff-links for the price of morning coffee, lonesome old whores were walking their breedless dogs, the crippled beggars squeezed out happy music, the children of God knows who—Miguel and Joshua and Patrick—flipped pennies at the wall.

It was a long day's walk and the old man's mention of Eighth Avenue might well have been a figure of speech. Tully put his question for about the thirtieth time just when the lights were going on outside the shop. The man behind the counter—a great flabby lump whose face had the grayness of nightfall in it—opened his mouth and closed it. Then he shrugged.

Tully repeated his question, adding: "Seven decorations in all, including the Croix de Guerre and the Congressional Medal of Honor."

"I know," the man said wearily. "I can tell you the why

of all of them, what he did to get 'em and how he got some of 'em for things which he didn't do."

Tully permitted himself a little sigh. "A talkative old fellow, eh?"

"A salesman, he should've been a salesman. You know why he talked, don't you?"

"More money?"

"That's it, my friend. Five dollars worth of tin and alloy and forty-five bucks of talk. I'm a sucker for talk."

He was a sucker for good custom, too, Tully thought. He must have had the General's decorations in and out many a time. The General might talk up the loan, but there were no odds at all on his chance of talking down the interest rate. "Did he give you much talk last Friday?"

"I got the talk when he brought them in. I got abuse when he'd take them out. He'd curse me out for a usurer, a flesh-bleeder. I wish you could hear the words, some of them I never heard, a foreign language."

"Did he give you the treatment Friday?" Tully persisted, having in mind the old man's reported abuse of the desk clerk.

"Nope. You see he didn't come in for them himself. It was his girl friend."

"That's interesting," Tully said. "I've been wanting to meet her."

"Yeah? She ain't so much, not for a man of his . . . but what the hell? I used to think he was a four-flusher. Then he'd come in here, and by Chris', he did sound genuine."

"He was," Tully said patiently.

"I know. I read in the papers all about him. The real thing."

"Tell me about the girl friend. Do you know her?"

The big man settled himself on a stool behind the counter, maneuvering his bottom on it to get comfortable. Tully was aware of the ache in his own feet. "No, but I've seen her around, I think."

"You mean without the General?"

"Maybe, but I don't know where. What I mean is, maybe she's an ex-singer, something like that, see?"

"Could be she is," Tully said. "Got a name for her? Did she sign a receipt?"

The pawnbroker shook his head. "Cash, merchandise, tickets. No signatures needed. That's household finance stuff. We're specialists. She had the ticket, she got the medals."

Tully at least got a good description of the woman. It tallied well with the hotel clerk's. "What time was she in?"

"Along about now. I have to put the lights on special in the window, and I was up there by the switch when she came in. I saw her outside looking up at the number first."

Tully looked at his watch. Six-twenty.

"What did you think you were going to get from her?" Tully asked. "Or did you know her from having been in before with the General?"

"That was her first time, I think." The big man rubbed his chin and you could hear the scrape of his hard thumb on the stubble of beard. "Funny, you ask that. I got a beautiful watch here. It came in a week ago, a guy from out of town, green, scared. I figured she came to get it for him. Class, you see. Whatever she was, she had class. Not enough maybe for a general. But class."

"Just the same," Tully drawled, "you figured her to be . . . whatever she was."

"Oh sure."

"Would you say she was worried? Upset?"

"Not a care in the world, I'd say. Looked all around. Inquired what I fed the parakeet."

Tully noticed the bird for the first time. It would be a safe conjecture then, that the General's mistress was mistress also to a parakeet. Nothing at all so far indicated her a woman capable of violence.

"How much was the ticket? Have you got that on the books?"

The big man heaved himself up and went to his ledger. He found the page and ran a pudgy finger along the entries. "Forty-three dollars and fifty cents—including interest." He closed the ledger. "And I tell you what she paid it out of—a hundred dollar bill."

That was no great surprise. It merely toted up the General's pocket money to a thousand dollars. "Anything else you remember about her?"

"She asked me if the bird talked. I said I wouldn't have a bird around which talked, meaning it double, you see. She caught on. She gave me a kind of wink. Real soft and southern lady, she was. 'Mine always says the proper thing,' she said, and going out she said: 'good evenin'.'"

It was downright disgusting to see this hunk of a man go mushy talking about a woman, Tully thought. He thanked him for his cooperation and clapped his hat on.

"Good evenin'," the big one called after him in a mock southern accent. Tully looked back from the door. The pawnbroker was churning with laughter.

Something, nothing. Something, nothing. The words kept time with his footfalls. He took a cab back to the office, and there, called up for the tracer on the license number Helene Joyce had got at the funeral.

"Sorry, Tully. Somebody goofed on you. There's no such number issued by the state."

Tully sat back and thought about that. Mrs. Joyce was a competent woman. But this was the second license number taken in this business that might have had great relevance: a drunk had memorized the license on the black limousine that took The Rock on his last mile, and there was no such number. Somebody was using plates of his own manufacture for these special occasions. And then there was the round-faced gentleman with the fading sunburn: he had put the finger on the General outside Minnie's that night, saying he was Johnny Rocco. He drove the limousine in which a fair blonde lady attended the General's funeral. Maybe they wouldn't add up yet, but you could count 'em: one, two, three.

Jasper Tully enjoyed his dinner.

28

It was a strange, empty house, the Jarvis home in Nyack, full of clutter and petty chores. They were all her duty, Mrs. Norris said, but she heaved a great sigh of regret when Jimmie and Helene drove off to the city early in the morning. At the gate they turned back, and Mrs. Norris retreated in haste from the window not to be caught at it.

"Mrs. Joyce would be pleased to have you stay over tonight, if you don't mind a small room," Jimmie said from the door.

"Thank her very much," Mrs. Norris said, "If my obligations permit it, I'd be obliged."

It made the morning of tedious chores tolerable, and the truth was that she would have been glad to squeeze into a mousehole to spend the night in the city. She talked to the painter who wanted far too much money to redo the General's rooms, and God knew, they needed redoing. The painter knew it, too, which was why he was standing by his price. She began sorting the household bills which she was in the habit of going over before giving to Jimmie to pay. The phone bill puzzled her—not that this was unusual—but there were two calls listed to her sister's exchange in Brooklyn on the same day, March fourteenth, the day before she had ridden in with the General. She could remember the call to Mag to see if she would be home. Well, the Nyack telephone company was not the most reliable in the world. It was one of the last stands of the old-fashioned system, depending more on the human element . . . and they were all very human, the Nyack operators.

Again the feeling of having been over an identical conversation! She picked up the phone and asked for the supervisor, watching the while as the gardener trudged into the house and over the kitchen floor with his muddy boots.

He would not do that in his own house, she'd wager. "Do you have to come in in your shoes?" she cried, covering the phone.

"Would you have me come in on my head?"

"Oh, very clever. There's a mop in the pail by the sink and you can just wipe the floor after yourself going out."

The man clapped his hat on his head. "I found these all over the place by the east beds," he said, and flung a handful of muddy, rusting pen nibs on the table before her.

"What do I want with them?"

He was forever complaining of the things people threw in his garden beds; cigarettes and matches, nails and buttons always seemed to be turning up there. Ordinarily she had a measure of sympathy with him, but this morning his trail of mud over the floor and the smear of it on her polished table set her near to screaming: "Get them out of here, Mr. Turpel, do you hear me!"

"Yes, madam." That was the Nyack supervisor. "Can I help you?"

"You can indeed," Mrs. Norris said, her wrath now compounded. "Whoever was making out the bill to Mr. James Ransom Jarvis was seeing double again, and it's not the first time. We are billed for two calls to Esplanade exchange, Brooklyn. Now it's my own sister who lives there and it was myself that made the call . . ."

"One moment, please. . . ."

Mrs. Norris waited and watched.

The gardener brushed the fistful of mud into his pocket; he grabbed the mop and without wringing it out dragged it over the bricks after him to the door where he left it in a puddle of its own making and slammed the door behind him.

"Are you sure, madam, there was but one call?"

"I am a careful woman with money, miss, and I would not make two calls where one would do."

"Very well, madam, we shall make the adjustment."

"Thank you very much." She then debated calling the Robinsons to inquire after her sister and say she would be over in the morning. She decided against it. This time she would surprise them. If Mag were only a little sick, she would be glad to see her; if she was very ill, she wouldn't care, and so far as Mr. Robinson was concerned, Mrs. Norris didn't care.

29

Jimmie read the item in Lem Python's column twice:

". . . One thing sure, if a certain young bachelor about town is elected governor it shouldn't hurt our relations with Great Britain. Things already seem to have been très intime with a branch of the royal household. Been that is, as in bean, old bean in fact . . ."

He made himself walk slowly out to the hall to the old-fashioned water-cooler and drink a cupful of water in the hope it would cool his temper. A remarkable thing had happened that morning when he entered the office: the senior partners had come to see him, to shake his hand. Nor was it all sympathy. With his father's passing, they looked upon him in a new capacity. He was now the head of an old family, the last survivor of the direct line, two hundred years American. No small responsibility, the honor of such a family, and now it was all his. They expected big things of him, Johnson, Wiggam and Jarvis did, and if he were not successful in his candidacy for governor, it would make no difference to them—so long as he conducted a dignified campaign.

Lem Python's column was just the place to establish dignity. So it was out, wherever it came from. His wartime escapade had been well observed by some camera eye. Madeline Barker's? He could think of no other. He was tempted to call her and blast her from there to the United Kingdom. He did not get the chance: she was waiting outside his office for him when he returned, and she was carrying a copy of *The Standard,* open to "The Python Pit."

Without a word they went to a conference room—the partners did not approve women in the private offices—and Madeline spread the newspaper on the table.

She was very formal. "We are going to have to go into this, Mr. Jarvis."

"I should think we are," said Jimmie. "You might at least have put it in good English for him."

"You think *I* gave it to him, Jimmie?"

"That had crossed my mind, Madeline. You've fed him before—to your own purpose, haven't you?"

"Of course."

Jimmie folded his arms. "Tell me, Madeline—from the shoulder—what do you think of me as a candidate?"

"From the shoulder—I think we could have done better." She looked him straight in the eyes, saying it.

It might have come from the shoulder, but Jimmie felt it in the pit of his stomach. "To what ends would you go to see me disqualified before the convention?"

"If this item in Python's column is true, I don't think I shall have to go very far, Jimmie."

"A trial balloon—is that it?"

A quiver of anger ran through her penciled brows. "Do you have two phones on one line here?"

Jimmie brought them from the cupboard and plugged them in.

"I shall try to get him on the phone, and I want you to listen." She gave the switchboard operator an unlisted phone number, and in immediate return, over the sound of dialing got part of a conversation: "So I says to him it looks like a clotheshanger, and he says to me: go to . . ." The circuit was closed. A moment later Python himself answered.

"Lem, this is Madeline Barker. Where did you get the story?"

"What's the matter, honey? Your personality boy threatening to sue? Let him."

"This is important to me, Lem."

"Don't you think it's worth something to ole Lem Python? A scoop is a scoop, baby. I crawl for 'em, remember?"

"Confidentially, Lem," she pleaded.

"Baby . . . come around some time when you're on one side or the other. You're getting a little too old to do the splits in public."

Jimmie heard the phone click and cradled his own. Madeline put the receiver slowly into place. It was a good act, Jimmie thought—if it was an act. "What did all that mean?" he asked.

"It means that Lem Python is a foul-mouthed, double-dealing bastard," she said, with shocking directness. She moved to the window overlooking Trinity Churchyard. "Can I go back to the headquarters and say you deny the whole thing, Jimmie?"

"You cannot. You and headquarters can ignore it as I intend to do."

"You can't ignore him, Jimmie!"

"Maybe you can't . . . I can."

Suddenly Miss Barker was in tears. Jimmie had to go to her. It was the only thing a gentleman could do, pat her on the shoulder, make soothing noises. Someone had called tears a woman's last line of defense, he thought. It was his own opinion that it was her best offense.

"Oh, Jimmie," she wailed, "it's so peaceful down there."

All that was down there that was peaceful was the cemetery, with the downtown traffic thundering by it.

"Too noisy," Jimmie said.

She looked at him, drying some not very wet tears. "You are an enigma," she said.

"An enigma and an egghead," he mused aloud. "I don't really think my name will ever reach the convention."

"Not unless you deny that story . . ."

Jimmie shook his head.

"Then let's work out some way between us of avoiding a direct answer."

"Why?"

"You can't ignore it, Jimmie."

"I can."

"Stop being so damned superior!"

This was a very interesting development, Jimmie

thought, watching her expose the raw edges of her temper. "Superior to whom, Madeline? To Python? I think I am. But then at the moment, I can't think of anyone inferior to him."

"I can," Madeline said, "if murder is worse than scandal. Right now, James Jarvis, I could murder you myself."

Jimmie was about to make a mistake and he knew it, but he plunged ahead as though fate had ordained it. "You have intimated a couple of times, my dear, some highly personal observations of my private life. I think the time has come for you to tell the truth and shame Lem Python, shall we say?"

She sat down and crossed a lovely pair of legs. "No lady could do that, Jimmie. What I will do though—you have my word that any confidence you give me will be respected."

"By whom?" Jimmie said. She was too damn eager.

"You are becoming a vast bore with your petty secrets, and your late carnivorous father. Be a man again, Jimmie. Speak up. There is no disgrace in having been one."

Jimmie strode across the room, glimpsing the half-open door, and marking that no one was visible from the angle at which he reached Madeline. He caught her chin beneath his thumb and forefinger, practically lifting her bodily from the chair by it; he kissed her full and hard upon the mouth, and then dropped her.

"You don't know a blasted thing about me, Miss Barker," he said then.

"Nothing except what you have taught me this moment, Mr. Jarvis."

That, he thought, was the truth. Conscience was no guide whatsoever in his case. "Yes?" he said, for she was looking pensive.

"Would you like to know something Lem taught me in one of his gentler moments? Always act as though you know something. Nine times out of ten you'll flush a skeleton."

"That does sound like one of his gentler moments," Jimmie said.

He took her to the elevator. To a problem which might very well prove legal he had used an approach that the partners would certainly disapprove. But they had a lifetime, nay, generations, and he had less than a month before the state convention.

30

Tully's call for information had gone out to all the cab companies, and to the garages where most of the privately owned taxis were serviced.

By Tuesday noon he had two responses. He had the men come in ten minutes apart. The first driver accounted picking up the General on Third Avenue and Fifty-fifth Street, Thursday night last at ten-thirty.

"Kind of breathy, you know, pantin', the old man was," the cabbie summed up his impression. "Said somethin' about not bein' able to take excitement anymore. Oh, and he asked me if I was married. 'Sure,' I says, 'six kids.' 'Ah-hah,' he says, 'that's how to keep 'em in their place. Give 'em plenty of kids to tie 'em down.' So I says, 'It don't give me much freedom neither, six kids.' 'True,' he says. 'All too true.' Then after a while, maybe Forty-second Street and Fourth, he leans up to ask me something like: did I ever want to be a cad. I didn't understand him, a cad. Who says a cad in this country? So I says: 'A what?' 'A sonofabitch,' he says. 'Oh, sure,' I says, 'but it don't do me no good, tryin' to be. When I don't try I do fine at it.'" The cabbie shrugged. "He just laughed. Good-natured old guy."

"How was the tip?" Tully asked.

"Nothin' special."

"Did he have a bag or anything like that?"

"Yeah. Matter of fact, gettin' out he says somethin' like: I better not leave this. Meanin' it was valuable. I mean that's what I thought."

And that was about the sum of cabbie-number-one's contribution. The detective filled in another space in his time-table for the General, adding:

Thursday. Mar. 15, 10:30 PM—Third Ave. and 55th took cab.

The conversation was set to the same tune, Tully thought, as the General played later with Webster Toll at the club bar, only in a different key.

Tully asked the second cabbie to sit down at his desk. A clerk had already taken his personal statistics. The detective looked sharply at him when he explained his observation point. He had been sitting in his cab, front man in the hackstand outside the Mulvany Hotel, when the General and his friends drove up in a black limousine.

"A black limousine?" Tully repeated.

"Yes, sir. A funny looking character, the chauffeur, his face looked like his backside, if you know what I mean. No expression."

Tully thought it was just one more description of that one, and on the whole, as vivid as any. He nodded his head. "Go on."

"Well, he jumps out, runs around and fair-to hoists the old man out where the other two are waitin' to help him. One under each arm. Brother, was the old man gone." The cabbie whistled.

"Gone?"

"Legs like rubber hoses."

Tully leaned forward and put his finger on the cabbie's chest. "Think about this, man: was it an act?"

"I'd say it was more an act than real, mister. Nobody could be that far gone and talkin'."

"What did he say?"

"Well, sir, I heard some of the damnedest cussin' ever lighted up Fifth Avenue. And I'll tell you, I felt real sorry for the little lady. She was shushin' him, and makin' all kinds of sympathic clucks. And I'll tell you, mister, she didn't look like an old hen type. I wouldn't be surprised she was actin' too. Could've been. Looked like a actress. Oldtimer maybe. Boop-oopidoop, or whatever that was, diamonds are a girl's last friend, you know?"

"I know," Tully said.

"I got out to give 'em a hand, hold the door, something like that? Sitting looking all day at the rear bumpers of hacks, cars, busses, you don't get a show like that was. Boy, that chauffeur was pushing my chest in in a minute. The other guy, helping the old man in, he took some money out of his pocket, give it to the chauffeur to give me, and says 'Thanks just the same,' to me. D'you know what that bloated buzzard did? He looked at the bill. Whatever it was, he put it in his own pocket and gave me fifty cents. I'd like to've bounced it on the sidewalk in front of him. But I didn't. He wasn't the kind you monkey around with, I'll tell you."

Tully nodded. "How long did he wait for them to come out?"

"He didn't. Got in, drove away. Clean. You can tell when somebody's got to poke around the block a half hour."

"No reason for you to've noticed his license, I suppose."

"Jersey," the cabbie said. "that's all I noticed."

"How did you figure it?"

"Well, sir," said the cabbie, "I just thought to myself, the poor, old bastard. He's just been rolled for everything he's got, except what's inside him. I figured him to've gone to one of them joints in New Jersey. Girls, gambling, the works. When it was all over, the boss, I figured, got his stooge to drive him home, that's Moon-face. The other two, I don't know. Maybe they picked him up here and took him over there, figuring a cut. Then again, maybe she got him, working alone, and when he passed out, this other guy was her steady boy friend. Sharp, her own class he was."

"Interesting," Tully said. "You're a pretty hep boy. I'll recommend you for the force if you ever want to put your cab to pasture."

"You mean it?"

Tully thought about it further. "As a matter of fact, I do." There was something very canny in the lad's story, he was sure. It came closer to the truth as he thought he could smell truth, than any tale he'd heard so far. "But now, how could the old man've been rolled if he wasn't drunk? If he was pretending, like you thought?"

"I didn't think he was pretending till you put it up to me, sir," the young cabbie said after a moment's thought.

"You know what I'd like you to do for me now?" Tully said. "Take a pencil and paper and write out all the curse words you heard. Don't make any up, just the ones you remember."

The cabbie grinned. "A pleasure."

Later, when he compared the testimony, he saw that it pretty well tallied with the hotel employees' statements: the only difference being, that the cabbie didn't use abbreviations.

Tully called his friend, the psychiatrist. The subject of hypnosis was less likely to use the language proposed to him by the hypnotist than to fall back on his own. This was New York street talk, Tully thought. The General might not find it offensive, but the detective just didn't think his tongue would curl round it easy. The method might be like him, but the substance wasn't. Not quite it wasn't. The General had used his own style many times upon the pawnbroker, and this wasn't it.

The detective looked at his watch. He had enough time to brief the D.A. and do one more stretch of legwork before driving uptown to pick up Mrs. Norris.

The legwork, merely a figure of speech this time, since he knew where he was going, took him to King's Mart on Forty-third Street. August Fowler had said he equipped himself there for his sudden fishing trip. It might be a lousy pun, Tully thought, but fishy was the word for an urge to go on a sporting expedition such as you had never gone on before, and to do it on the morning after a client of considerable distinction is come upon dead. Especially when you were one of the last people to have seen him, certainly the last to do business with him. Just how fishy it was, Tully hadn't realized until he asked the manager of King's Mart, who had himself waited on Fowler, how much equipment the agent had bought.

"It came to eight hundred and ten dollars," the man said.

Tully rolled his tongue around the phrase. He could almost taste it, a pleasurable bit to a detective who was tasting his first real substance. "Eight hundred and ten dollars, with tax, I presume."

"With tax."

"He wasn't after perch, was he?"

"Bass, I believe," the manager said, not sharing Tully's pleasure at all. "He said he expected to do quite a bit of fishing. Health, he said. Better than doctor bills."

"Weren't you impressed with a purchase like that?"

"Only enough to wait on him myself," the manager said. Tully thought he might have humor after all. But it was said in deadly earnest. "He wanted advice."

"Do the bass really run in March?"

"They do off North Carolina."

"Pretty cold though, isn't it?"

"I equipped him for that."

"I'll bet," Tully said. "And he took it all with him, paying cash. Or was it a check?"

"Cash, sir."

"Would you've taken his check?"

"Certainly. He's a reputable business man."

"I guess he is at that," Tully drawled. "But didn't you have any thoughts about how a man would be carrying that much cash?"

"Thoughts like that are valuable only to a policeman," the manager said.

"Touché," said Tully, "or whatever it is they say in France. If I was to ask you now to give a guess as to where he got it, what would you say?"

The man shrugged. "Gambling, perhaps, which is no sin in my books."

"I think he was gambling all right," Tully said. "I think maybe he was gambling that me or somebody like me would be coming in here to talk to you. How much did he pay you to lay it on juicy and thick, just like you've done now?"

The man lost neither his temper nor his color. "I will give you the duplicate of his sales slip, officer, and I will put at your disposal our price lists. You can add it up, and I will stake my honor on your computation."

"Do that," Tully said. "Send it to the District Attorney's office marked for me."

Tully stalked out of the shop. He didn't like showing his temper, but he didn't like to miss by as wide a margin as he now feared he had in accusing the manager of consciously collaborating Fowler's story.

The King's man was incorruptible, of course, Tully mulled the words to himself, checking his notebook in the car for something else in Fowler's story. He was going fishing with Wilson Dram, the writer. Tully drove up to Forty-seventh Street and consulted a dear little wisp of an Irish friend at Brentano's. Five minutes later he knew who Dram's publisher was, and a phone call there revealed that Dram had a home in Briarwood, Connecticut.

Tully drove to East Side Homicide, the nearest police facilities. Then he played a hunch. He got in touch with the First National Bank of Briarwood, whistling softly while he waited. Even while he passed the amenities with the cashier, however, his mood changed; he realized that something was wrong with his theory. He tried it anyway.

"Wilson Dram does have an account with you people?"

"A substantial one, sir," the cashier said.

"When I put in this call," Tully explained then, "I was going to ask you if he by any chance made a substantial withdrawal, say a thousand dollars, on the morning of March seventeenth. Then I realized that was Saturday. You're closed then, aren't you?"

"Yes, sir."

"So he couldn't have made it then?"

"I'm afraid not, sir."

"Just for the hell of it, check yesterday and today, will you?"

Tully watched the second hand round the clock four times.

"Mr. Tully? Nothing, sir. But I've just talked with Mr. Ryan, our president, a personal friend of Mr. Dram's. He would like to speak to you."

"Put him on," Tully said.

"I speak in absolute confidence," Ryan started.

"A policeman's confidence can't be very absolute, Mr.

Ryan," the detective said. "But I don't think this information is going to hurt your client."

"I suppose you could get an order anyway," the banker said.

"Real easy," said Tully.

"Dram made a personal loan of all I could give him early Saturday morning. Got me out of bed for it about seven-thirty. He wanted a thousand. I could give him six hundred and did. I expect he approached one or two other people for the rest. He said a friend of his was in trouble."

"He's going to be, Mr. Ryan. You can be pretty sure of that. Thanks very much. Just keep my call to yourself for a while, and I'll do the same about where I got my information."

"I would deeply appreciate that," the banker said.

Tully had been going to get in touch with Dram. He decided there was not much point to it for the present. Dram would only lie—at least until he went under oath for his friend, Fowler.

So, he thought, driving uptown to the Rockland bus station, when August Fowler learned that General Jarvis was dead, he had found it absolutely imperative to alibi himself with an expenditure of a near thousand dollars, and quick. His own bank account, wherever he kept it, and an hour's exploration should discover that, would no doubt show a cash withdrawal of ten one hundred dollar bills sometime between ten a.m. and bank closing, Friday. The General was still in pocket near a thousand dollars when he died, Friday. Not for anything, did Augie Fowler want to be connected with the General's pocket money.

Why not?

31

Mrs. Norris had a few things of her own to say when she got off the bus with the assistance of a hand from the gallant Jasper Tully. They both started to talk at once, then both were silent at once, and both then broke into laughter.

In the car, Mrs. Norris took from her purse a piece of ribbon and handed it to the detective. The name of the shop from which it came was stamped on it: *Eric's Flowers* . . . and with a number on Third Avenue, New York.

"Aren't you interested in how I came by it?" she said in a small huff when Tully merely grunted.

"Oh, I am, I am." The devil a person was interested in how he came by his information, as long as he got it. But sure it was his business. "Forgive me, dear lady."

"Well, I reported to you on the telephone, Mr. Tully, the vulgar floral piece I took to have come from *that* woman?"

"You did," said Tully. "Very observant of you."

"I knew it ne'er came from Rockland County," she continued, "whatever we lack up there, we've taste. Well then, the more I thought of it through the morning, and knowing yesterday to've been a bit crisp, I wondered if the florist wouldn't have wrapped something round it to protect the flowers from frost in transit."

"Worthy of Holmes himself," cried Tully.

"Will you stop it, man!" Mrs. Norris fanned her face. "So I called up Mr. Hanson who's by way of being a friend of mine—especially at Christmas. He's Sanitary Commissioner, you understand. He drove out himself to the refuse baskets near the cemetery gate. And sure enough, he found a whirl of papers and this ribbon inside it."

"A valuable piece of detection, Mrs. Norris, and that's not flattery. You may have put us closer to her than we've been to date. She has a parakeet, by the way."

"A guady wench, Mr. Tully. I'm shocked even at the General."

"But simple tastes," Tully speculated.

"You call that horseshoe of a wreath simple?"

"I'd forget about that, but don't you see, Mrs. Norris, that was by way of her last tribute to him. It was nothing she asked for herself."

"That's so," Mrs. Norris said thoughtfully, and glanced at him sideways.

"Well. I happen to know a very nice little restaurant in that neighborhood. If you'll take your dinner with me, Mrs. Norris, we'll kill two birds with a single sling. What do you say?"

"I'll have to let Master Jamie know where I am."

"Oh, we'll do better than that. I've to report a thing or two to him myself, and they've asked us for a drink, you know, at Mrs. Joyce's."

"Oh, I know Mrs. Joyce all right. I'm spending the night there, her guest mind you."

"A lovely woman," Tully said. "Now first we have a bit of investigating to do."

"Both of us?"

Tully nodded. "We're going to stop at the office of General Jarvis' literary agent." And on the way he accounted his information on August Fowler.

32

Tully stood, hat in hand, beside Mrs. Norris before Fowler's receptionist. He was, even stooping a little, head, shoulders, and almost an elbow taller than the dumpy little bundle of dignity beside him. Mrs. Norris' hands were composed like a queen's, over the leather bag. And the detective wondered how Fowler's lacquered blonde would place him and the lady. He had no intention of properly identifying himself until he could strike Fowler a surprise blow.

"I'm sorry, Mr. Fowler isn't in," she said, not even amusement in her eyes.

"When will he be back, ma'am?" Tully rolled his hat brim round in his hand, heightening the pose he had struck of a country lad on his first city venture.

The blonde shrugged. "Five o'clock possibly."

"What do you think, child?" he said to Mrs. Norris, his long face solemn. "Havin' come all this way, we ought to see him."

All Mrs. Norris could manage was to nod her head.

The switchboard needed attention. The receptionist snapped them a smile, and attended a call . . . Her voice had the sound of having attended similar calls all afternoon. "Yes, Mr. Python . . . I'll tell him, Mr. Python. As soon as he comes in, sir. . . . Mr. Python, I am not lying to you. There are people here in the office right now waiting for him . . ."

Tully and Mrs. Norris had taken chairs side by side. "What kind of name is that, Python?" said Mrs. Norris.

"He likes to be called a snake," Tully said. "Haven't you ever heard of the columnist, Lem Python?"

"Oh him," she said with withering scorn.

"It's a most peculiar world we live in, Mrs. Norris. Sometimes I think there's people around today who regret not having been born in the Garden of Eden just so they could commit original sin."

The receptionist broke one phone connection and opened another, apparently to an inner office. "Mr. P. again, Julie. What do I tell him next? Boiling . . . oh, honey, I want to live. I'll give him to you next time . . ."

Again she stretched a rubbery smile at Tully and Mrs. Norris and snapped it off. "I don't really think Mr. Fowler is going to be able to see you folks today," she said. "Why don't you make an appointment and come back tomorrow?"

Mr. Tully got to his feet, hat clutched to chest. "Do you think we ought to stay in New York, child. Even tonight?"

Mrs. Norris opened her mouth and closed it. She could not play the game. And that merely provoked Tully into greater exaggeration.

"Wouldn't you like to tell me your business? Maybe I could help you," the blasé blonde suggested.

That was exactly the cue Mr. Tully wanted. "Well, I tell you, miss," he drawled. "My sister and me were fixin' to write a book. We get to see all kind of people in our business, you understand?"

"What business are you in?" she said, and stretched her mouth over a yawn.

"We run a H house . . . flowers, you know, a hot-house."

At least, he thought, he had spoiled a good yawn. She looked him over then, and apparently decided he was genuine.

"I don't really think Mr. Fowler would be the agent for you folks. But why don't you go home and call him up tomorrow morning?"

"Early?"

"Very early, say eleven o'clock."

By the time they reached the elevator, Mrs. Norris allowed herself to giggle.

"I'd like to have seen her expression if I'd given her the D.A.'s card," Tully said.

"That lass lost her expression with her virtue," Mrs. Norris said.

Tully sighed. "No doubt, no doubt."

33

"Yes," Jimmie said, pacing back and forth before the terrace window, "I kissed her. Furthermore she liked it."

"But of course she liked it," Helene said sweetly. "I told you she was in love with you. Furthermore, if you really want to be governor, you're going to have to kiss her again and again, having started it."

Jimmie stopped in his tracks. "It wasn't so hard to do, you know. And it's a hell of a lot better than smacking babies."

Helene gave a vigorous stir to the martinis. "Okay, darling. You're on loan till after elections. I'll get more work done."

"Nice," Jimmie said, tracing his finger about a granite nude. "I haven't seen this before, have I?"

"You have. I'm going to put it in the garden. It's weatherable."

"Very," Jimmie murmured. "What do you mean, I'm on loan? Stop treating me like something you've carved out of stone."

"Pygmalion-femina." Helene refilled his glass, then touched hers to it. "Or perhaps it will be best after all if I avail myself of Judge Turner's fellowship."

The doorbell sounded at the front of the house. "That will be our young romantics," Helene said, and went to admit Mrs. Norris and Tully.

Jimmie was enjoying a mood of liquid gold, momentary and transient. And strictly out of Helene's martini mixer. But, God help him, he thought, why had he ever sought to spoil a beautiful friendship by talk of a marriage neither of them really wanted? Helene at least was no hypocrite. He was mouthing the catechismal lines of Mrs. Norris. The little housekeeper came in wreathed in smiles, and he would have sworn she would be of disapproving mien. Tully was a good influence.

Both she and Tully took their whiskey neat, while the detective summed up for Jimmie his work of the last two days. Jimmie would not take to the notion of hypnotism at all, and Helene sided with him.

"Got a better explanation?" Tully said, somewhat irked. He had not come easily by the notion himself.

"Who hypnotized him then?" said Jimmie. "The character who brought him in to the hotel? Father was not the type to submit himself to nonsense. He liked his whiskey straight, his women submissive, and his money in cash. Excuse my frankness, Mrs. Norris."

She merely nodded, intent on something at which she was gazing.

Tully switched then to a discussion of Fowler, and while he was talking Jimmie became aware that the housekeeper's attention was focused on the male nude he had commented on earlier. Now and then, she glanced from it to him, and back to it again. Jimmie realized what was going on in her mind. The piece was sculpted, hands behind the head, knees drawn slightly up, ankles crossed. It was a hell of a position, but Jimmie managed to take it. Tully was reading from notes. Helene saw the situation between Mrs. Norris and her employer, the man she had raised from rompers, and covered her mouth with a glass. Sixty seconds passed; Jimmie was aching. Then Mrs. Norris saw his position.

She gave a little "oh" and began to fan herself vigorously.

"You were saying, Jasper?" Jimmie said, springing loose his limbs. Helene turned her back.

Tully looked up from his notes. "I was saying that if Fowler denied giving your father a thousand dollars, if I were you, I'd get that diary back from him and take a good look at it."

"I intend to," Jimmie said. "I called him twice today, and no return call. I was going to ask you to take a hand."

"Mrs. Norris and I stopped there on our way. He wasn't in."

"But the girl in the office thought he might be back at five o'clock, didn't she?" said Mrs. Norris, having recovered herself.

"She changed her tune later. Remember?"

"Was that to us or was it to that Mr. Python on the phone?" said Mrs. Norris.

Jimmie leaped to his feet. "Wait a minute, wait! Python did you say?" Tully and Mrs. Norris nodded. "Go over that part for me slowly."

Tully recounted the receptionist's remarks. "My guess is, he was spittin' mad, the Python, at our Mr. Fowler."

"Was he?" Jimmie said, grinding the fist of one hand into the palm of the other. "Where do you think that diary is, Jasp?"

"If it was worth a thousand dollars cash to Fowler on Friday, and another thousand to hide under Saturday, I'd say it's in a safe someplace."

"Let's get a warrant."

"Well, I was thinking of that. But why not try it the easy way first—finding him and asking him for it? Could be, he'll show up in his office in the morning. My guess right now is it's Python he's ducking, not us."

"Did you see Python's column this morning, Jasp?"

"Can't really say I've ever read him."

Jimmie took the clipping of the column from his pocket and gave it to Tully. "Might as well read it aloud," he said, and went to the window overlooking the garden.

Tully read the item and whistled softly.

"Do you think that in some way your father was responsible for that, Jimmie?" Helene asked.

Jimmie raised his fists to heaven on the odd chance that the old gentleman had made it. "He's one of two possibilities, and right now I'd nominate him, sure."

Mrs. Norris finished her drink and got to her feet. "I'd say one of three, Master James," she said with stiff formality.

"Three?"

"Aye, yourself is one also."

There was no denying her Scots righteousness, Jimmie thought. And unlike Madeline Barker, she could not be converted by a kiss. Not by his at least. Jimmie let his eyes appeal to Tully.

Tully merely looked at his pocket watch. "It's time for us to go out to our dinner, Mrs. Norris."

Jimmie took them to the door. When they were gone, he returned, massaged his chin with his thumb. "I guess myself *is* one also," he said, "for having got myself in so vulnerable a position."

"A lot of people were vulnerable during the war, Jimmie."

"While the generals died in bed," Jimmie said, misquoting a poem of that sentiment.

His eyes met Helene's for a moment. "Sorry," he said, "that was crass of me."

"Some people say martinis are depressants," Helene said. "Shall I put on the steak?"

34

"Duty first. Then we can relax," Mrs. Norris said, and then suddenly realized she was relaxing more with Mr. Tully than so short an acquaintance justified. Ah, but it was like the stress of wartime, and like war, it wasn't the circumstance you welcomed, but the distraction you found from it.

Mr. Tully, who might never have relaxed at all if he did the duties connected with his office first, consented at least to follow up Mrs. Norris' clue to the General's fair lady. He commenced their exchange with the florist by buying Mrs. Norris a single tea rose for her shoulder and a bit of green to cushion it. She was putting it on and Tully paying for it when she remembered Robbie and his quoting of Bobbie Burns . . . "My love is like a red, red rose."

"Oh there now," she said, "you've put me in mind of my brother-in-law."

"Is that good or bad?" said Tully, waiting his change.

"I don't know that it's bad, but it isn't good," she said. "I'll tell you about it later if you like."

The man behind the counter returned, and counted Mr. Tully his change. "I wonder," the detective said, "if you'd mind telling me about a floral piece you fixed yesterday morning early . . . You describe it, Mrs. Norris."

Mrs. Norris did, mostly with a great circular motion as though she were illustrating an angel's wings.

The man's eyes narrowed ever so slightly. He shook his head, "I don't think it came from here, madam."

Tully took the ribbon from his pocket and ran it through his fingers while he spoke. "Now nobody would fix more than one or two pieces like that in a lifetime, much less on a Monday morning."

The man lifted his head. "I'm sorry, sir, I don't remember fixing it."

Tully went on easily. "I'd guess maybe a lady bought it, an old customer who lives in the neighborhood, A good-natured woman, likes birds, an ex-show girl."

Mrs. Norris looked up. It was quite a picture Mr. Tully was drawing. She had not reached the "show girl" part of it in her own mind, but it fit in very neatly, she realized now. It was pleasant to admire a man as she was now admiring Jasper Tully. And there again she cautioned herself. For longer than some men's lifetimes, she had admired Mr. Robinson.

The florist shook his head steadily, and this in spite of the fact that his eyes took in the ribbon in the detective's hand.

"Do you have an assistant?" Tully asked.

"Only my wife. She relieves me at mealtime. And she would not have done up anything like you describe, believe me, sir."

"I'd like to," Tully said, and tried another approach before throwing the authority of his office into the persuasion. "I'll tell you who it was for. That might refresh your memory. It was for the funeral of General Ransom Jarvis. Does that help?"

The man squeezed the color out of his fingers. "I knew General Jarvis, if that's what you mean, sir."

"That'll do for now," Tully said. "Tell us about it."

"Not much to tell. He was in the habit of coming in once a week or so, and picking out a bouquet to take with him."

"Never sent them?" Tully asked.

"No sir. And just to show his authority, he was in the habit of plucking out a stem or two. 'Can't offend the lady,' he'd say."

"When was he in last?"

"Friday night—a little after five. He drove up in a cab and bought two dozen roses."

"You're sure of the time?" said Tully.

"I am. My wife was due at five o'clock and I was getting hungrier by the minute."

"Did he keep the cab waiting?"

"No sir."

"How much were the flowers?"

"Eight dollars."

"What did he pay them out of—what size bill?"

"A five and three singles, but he did ask if I could change a hundred dollar bill."

"That's what I figured," Tully said.

He could afford a cab but he walked from here, the detective thought. It must put his lady within—say—a block or two.

Mrs. Norris cleared her throat. "Had he been your customer for a long time, sir?"

"Off and on, a good many years. I remember him in uniform."

"Do you now?" she said, in a tone that took the pleasure out of the florist's reminiscence.

Tully edged around the matter for a moment to let the man's hackle settle, and then asked: "Does the lady ever buy flowers herself from you?"

"I tell you, sir," the man said with exaggerated patience. "I don't even know the lady. This might be her for all of me." He indicated Mrs. Norris.

"Well for all of me, it might not!" she cried.

"Didn't he ever make conversation with you? Did he never refer to the woman at all?" said Tully.

"He had a saying," the florist said. "I'm trying to think of it. Something like: 'Blossoms for my Blossom.' That's not right, but something like that. Maybe her name was Rose!" Then he shook his head, turning down his own conjecture. "I'm sorry, officer."

"Don't mention it." Then Tully snapped: "That big funeral wreath—how much did the gangster pay you for it?"

The shopkeeper went a little pale, and his hand trembled when he picked up the ribbon Tully threw on the counter, but he stuck to his story. "I don't know what you're talking about."

Tully saluted him, the tip of his hat with the tip of his fingers, and let the matter stand. Outdoors he said to Mrs.

Norris: "I could have asked him to let me see his books. But it probably wouldn't show anything we don't know now. The wreath was bought there, all right, and by the big bag of cheese in the chauffeur's uniform. I don't really think the flower man knows anything except enough to be scared. And he is scared. That tells quite a lot, you see."

"Poor man," said Mrs. Norris.

"I told you we should've had our dinner first," said Tully.

"What will you do now?" Mrs. Norris said as they walked the few paces down Third Avenue and turned a corner, going in a door that said *Family Entrance.* She forgot her own question for a moment: "I haven't been in a family entrance for years!"

It was a fine old tavern-restaurant, with the smell of gravy and beer combined, white cloths on the table, pyramided napkins, thick plates and the best roast beef in New York, according to Mr. Tully. He excused himself for a moment, taking pen and notebook from pocket to make a few notations.

"Why, what will I do now? Cherchez la femme, as they say in France. We know quite a bit about her now. We know for example she'll be disposing of some poor faded roses soon, the last of a lovely crop. You might even call her 'The last rose of summer left blooming alone'." He sounded very mournful. "Except I don't think she's blooming alone. We also know she has the services of a chauffeured car, and one that might be intimately connected with the murder of a Brooklyn gangster."

The mention of Brooklyn again turned Mrs. Norris' thoughts to her own family. She confided to the detective her sudden concern for her sister.

"What does he do for a living, you brother-in-law?"

"He's a printer. And he's always been a fine provider, Mr. Tully. And there's times I really think it's my own imagination. I'd put it all down to that right now if I'd only been able to talk to Mag herself. But first she was out for a walk at eight in the morning, then she was sick of the stomach, then she was . . . well."

Tully nodded sympathetically. "The thing you should do is go out there without advance notice."

"I'm doing just that in the morning."

"Fine. I'll drive you over myself, for I've an errand there. Do you like your beef rare, Mrs. Norris?"

"Just so it doesn't kick me in the teeth," she said.

35

It was nine o'clock in the morning when the detective put her down at the corner a few doors from her sister's. There was no use rousing Mr. Robinson's curiosity about Mr. Tully by having him drive her up to the door. She climbed the front steps, noticing a half dozen cigarette stubs stamped out there, something Mag would not tolerate if she were herself. Mrs. Norris' heart beat the drum of alarm. She thrust herself forward with determination and tweaked the doorbell.

Mr. Robinson came through the hall from the kitchen in his shirt sleeves. He needed to open his mouth twice before he could say anything. Then he honeyed her with sweet talk.

"I want to see my sister, Mr. Robinson. That's all I ask."

"Dear Annie, ask anything you like." He drew her in the door and steered her down the hall with him, very neatly keeping her from entering the living room.

"Will you have a cup of tea with me first, and we'll go up together and wake her?" Mr. Robinson took his handkerchief from his pocket and wiped his hands vigorously—a very nervous habit, Mrs. Norris thought.

"I'll wait if she's sleeping," she said, and in the kitchen sat down to the tea he had been brewing as she came to the door. If all was not well, it would give her the sense of the house to see more of it, she thought, for somehow it was changed from when last she had been there.

"You look a bit peaked yourself, Annie. Have you not been sleeping?"

"With my eyes open, Mr. Robinson," she said.

He threw back his head and laughed so that the roof of his denture showed. She cast her eyes down, and stirred her tea; the man was acting daft.

"Excuse me a minute, Annie," he said, and slipped out the door into the front hall again.

She was of half a mind to follow him, but there was no sense in getting panicked. She drank the strong tea, and listened to the clock tick. The other morning Mag was out for a walk at eight, now she was still abed at nine. And the brief glimpse Mrs. Norris had got of the living room revealed the look of an all-night party, or at least occupancy by too many people. Aye, that was the whiff she got, stale smoke, cigars. She could remember it in the old days when the politicians would gather round Mr. James.

She took her teacup to the sink. A yellowed saucer showed where Mr. Robinson had had his breakfast, for she had noticed a bit of egg on the back of his hand where he had wiped his mouth on his way to admit her. She looked about now for eggshells, and found them in the garbage bucket. One egg only. But of course, Mag was still asleep.

The urge to know the truth became irresistible. She went out into the hall and up the stairs. He was in the living room, on the phone with someone. She could hear the rumble of his voice, but no words. He had shut the door. She could see the open bedroom door from the top step, the double bed gaping where someone had risen from sleep there.

"Mag?" she said softly.

No answer at all.

She went to the guest room then, for if Mag were ill, it was best to sleep alone. But the bed was as neat there as a walking stick. She hurried along then to Mag's sewing room at the other end of the upstairs. A studio couch, she remembered there, and the morning sun. She opened the door after ever so light a tap. Mag's sewing dummy stood fully dressed in a summer frock. It gave Mrs. Norris such a turn she let out a little moan and retreated into the hall. She had her hand on the railing to go downstairs, when Mr. Robinson spoke from the master bedroom.

"Are you sure you conducted a thorough search, Annie?"

She walked into the bedroom, her hands on her hips. "Where is my sister, Mr. Robinson?"

He was sitting on the corner of the bed, a bitter smile on his face. Suddenly he leaped to his feet and to the closet door. "Did you look in here?" he cried, flinging open the door.

Only a dress hung loose. After the start she had got from the dummy, Mr. Robinson's intended bit of cruelty was not even a bad joke. It left her unaffected.

"I'm warning you. I'll go to the police when I go out of this house if I don't see Mag."

"Where, where is the trusting friendship, Annie, that made us paragons among warring in-laws? Did I tell you Mag was up here? I did not. You leaped to your own conclusion. Come downstairs now. I'll put on my coat and we'll go up together. She spent the night with our next-door neighbor. The doctor has given her pills, you see, and I'd to entertain some customers here . . . Well, if she's awake she'll tell you, and if she's sleeping, you'll sit by her side and be her first waking vision."

Mrs. Norris went down the stairs with sodden humility. Either she was a great fool, or he took her for one—and she must be, not to know which was the case herself.

She was introduced to Mrs. Anders, who then put her hand on Mr. Robinson's arm. "She slept the night through like a baby."

Little she knew of babies, Mrs. Norris thought, if she was of the opinion they slept the night through. But there was Mag sitting up, a bed jacket about her shoulders, and a tray in her lap, and her eyes lighting up for a minute when she saw her sister.

"Look who I brought with my morning kiss, love," said Mr. Robinson, leaning over his wife, and whispering whatever else he had to say in her ear.

The light was gone from her eyes when he moved from between the women.

"Sit down, Annie," Mag said, more whining than ever. "I'm a bit weak from nerves, that's all."

"I was worried," Mrs. Norris said.

"Oh, and wasn't she, love? She was of the opinion I'd done away with you."

"He's very good to me, Annie," Mag said.

Mrs. Anders, a big woman, bounced into the room with a cup and saucer. "You'll have some tea from your sister's pot, Mrs. Norris."

Her own nerves were already jangling from the cup she had had at Mr. Robinson's, and she declined. The gesture, she thought, was made to show her that Mag's tea was tea and nothing else. They were trying to be wonderful tranquilizers, the lot of them. But when Mag gave her the tray, and remarked that she thought it was time she got up and dressed, Mrs. Norris had very little choice but to accept things as she saw them instead of as she had imagined them.

"I'm much obliged to you, Mrs. Anders," Robinson said, and then to Mrs. Norris. "You'll help her over if she needs it, I'm sure, and have a fine day together the two of you. I'll be at the shop if you want anything, Annie. Here's my card with the phone number."

Syrup ran no smoother than he did, but for the life of her she could not bring herself to apologize for mistrusting him. She looked at his card when he was gone:

Printing—old style and new
Quicker than you can say
Jack Robinson
493 Front St., Brooklyn, U.S.A.
MAin 3–6718

36

One of the puzzling things about the General's associates and activities the night before he died was the absence of fingerprints, complete and absolute, from the right door handle of his car. Someone had wiped them off. Which would seem to mean, Jasper Tully reasoned, that someone was in the car with him that day who anticipated trouble, and someone maybe whose fingerprints had a notable history.

He thought about this after leaving Mrs. Norris at her brother-in-law's, chiefly because he was on his way to see Johnny Rocco's man. In spite of Mrs. Norris' assertions to the contrary, he was not entirely convinced that the General might not have had an old-time association with The Rock which, just for the hell of it, he might have been reviving. There was something about the Twenties. Well, he was over sixty himself, Jasper Tully, and to dig out the few best years of his life, he would find them there. And you couldn't doubt that retired in the bloom of health, a man like the General would be bored. Having survived many dangers, he was likely to take risks that would shiver more timid men into their beds. No, he decided, it was not at all impossible for the General to have been in some sort of game with The Rock, a game in which he needed money quickly. Perhaps, when he found out Jimmie was headed for Albany, he decided to pull out, and had to buy his way . . . therefore the business deal with Fowler. Then something went awry. For The Rock, fatally awry. Was he, by any chance, hoisted on his own petard? Did he maybe get something intended for the General in that last ride from the bank? He had left the motor running in a low-slung sports car, something the General also drove.

All these things the detective turned over and round in his mind, and wondered then in summary, how close to the truth he had come in any one of them.

It was in the end, the moon-faced character, seen as the chauffeur of the General's lady friend, that made the link for Tully. If he should turn out now to be the deceased Johnny Rocco's bodyguard . . . Tully gave the revolver in his shoulder holster a pat, as though to assure himself of its company.

However, it was a man almost as tall as himself, and with a face lean-cheeked as a medieval monk's, who opened the double doors on Johnny's house to Tully. Rocco's man protested that he had never heard the name of General Jarvis in this house.

"Ask me questions," he said, "I'll prove it. I'll prove I tell you the truth. Anything about The Rock."

"Was he ever married?" Tully asked.

"No. No women. Not for a long time. I tell you how it was. During prohibition, he took the pledge, no drink. During the depression, he took the pledge, no women. That way he doesn't get into no trouble."

"Didn't he have any hobbies?" said Tully.

"Sure. Sports cars, absolutely authentic."

Tully thought about that for a moment. "Absolutely authentic what?"

"I tell you how it was." This punk, this gangster, spread out the most beautiful hands Tully had ever seen. "The Austin-Healey, you know?"

"I know. The one outside the bank."

Rocco's man nodded. "That one. Two in the whole world like it. Do you know who's got the other?" Tully shook his head. "English royalty. The Duke of Glower. Absolutely authentic."

Tully thought of the item in Python's column which suggested an intimacy between Jimmie and English royalty. He rubbed the back of his neck vigorously. "How do you know?"

The man shrugged. "I don't know, not me. I wouldn't know a Hillman Minx from a baby carriage. But The Rock knew. He used to slap me on the chest and say, 'Look at her, Slim. Me and the Duke of Glower got one.' And it was me personal had to bathe her."

"Wonderful," Tully growled. "You didn't happen to personal bathe a neat little Jaguar lately, did you? Say, the door handle on the right side?"

"Huh?"

Tully let it go. He left soon thereafter, the second door closing behind him slowly like the rising of a castle moat in a Hollywood spectacular. Maybe in the next such picture they could use a medieval monk named Slim.

He went then to see the officials at the bank where Johnny The Rock did his last business.

37

When August Fowler's blonde receptionist unlocked the office door in the morning she admitted Jimmie Jarvis as well as herself. It was a nice way to start the day, a client like this, well dressed, clean shaven, and up so early in the morning. Considering the mess he had got the whole office into, Mr. Fowler should find a gentleman like this some relief, too. She hinted every way she could to find out who he was.

Finally Jimmie said: "Remember that tall, skinny man who was in here yesterday, with a sweet little woman?"

The girl nodded, but you could almost see the lacquer spreading to her face.

"I'm their lawyer," Jimmie said. And that saved him from further conversation. He sat in the chair nearest the door, his face averted, and the moment Fowler had taken two steps into the room, Jimmie spoke his name. "I'm accustomed to the courtesy of having my calls returned," he said when the agent swung around.

"I'm sorry, Mr. Jarvis. I've been so damnably busy. Spring season, you know."

"For what, fishing?"

The agent flushed. "Come inside, eh?" He gave instructions to the girl about his calls and his secretary when she came in.

"Now," said Jimmie, as soon as the man reached his desk. "What kind of a game were you up to with my father?"

"It wasn't a game, I assure you."

"I think it was, something very confidential—like this item in Python's column."

"Your father, and I hate to say it of the dead, was a

conniving, double-crossing old gentleman. There was nothing he would not do for money."

"There were some things," Jimmie said, wishing to heaven he could think of least one. "What did you buy from him for a thousand dollars?"

Fowler folded his arms, as though to protect the truth in his breast. "Foolish of me to have tried to cover that up, wasn't it?"

"What did you buy?"

"I suppose you won't believe this. I merely loaned him the money against the publisher's advance when it came."

"You thought the diary was valuable?"

Fowler met Jimmie's eyes. "I thought he needed money that desperately. Early Friday afternoon he called me and offered me fifty percent of the diary for one thousand dollars. I got him the thousand—but declined more than the customary ten percent."

"How altruistic of you," Jimmie said with sarcasm.

"Funny—I thought you'd say something like that. Now listen to me, Jarvis—it wasn't necessary for me to tell you this at all. But here it is—sometime between ten a.m. when he was in my office and shortly after noon, he needed money quick and urgently. From our conversation that morning, I'd say it had to do with the Brooklyn gangster's death—Rocco. He went out of here in a fog when I told him about it."

A circle was always round, Jimmie thought. For all the haste and urgency, his father had stopped to buy his mistress flowers. "Ten one hundred dollar bills?" he asked.

Fowler nodded. "You asked me if I thought the diary that valuable. I did and do—if it's authentic. At the time I did not consider the thousand such a risk."

Jimmie thought about the word authentic. "Do you doubt its authenticity?"

"While your father was alive," Fowler said, "I felt no need for such doubts."

"In other words," said Jimmie, "when he was alive to make good—or pay the penalty—a thousand dollars was no risk."

"Precisely."

"Let me have the diary," Jimmie said slowly.

"Do you have one thousand dollars with you?"

"No, but I have the District Attorney's office within call."

Fowler shrugged. "And of course, you are an honest man, unlike your father. You see, I planned to exploit the book by feeding bits of it to the columnists. I confided this to your father. Little did I know that he would go from this office to that of Lem Python and do a bit of selling himself."

"Are you sure of that, Fowler?"

The agent waved his hands over his head. "Where else did it come from? Python showed me my release—unopened. That's what the diary's about, man, the interesting part of it—the amours of your ancestral President and a certain Lady Sylvia Mucklethrop while he was Ambassador to England."

Jimmie closed his eyes for a moment, and plainly before them he saw his father at the desk. . . . "Who is Sylvia?". . . . his face cherubic with mock innocence. "The monstrous villain," he whispered piously to himself.

Fowler stood at his window, his back to Jimmie.

"I suppose," Jimmie said then, "you put a dateline on your release and then accused Python of breaking it?"

"Exactly. How could I suspect an officer of the United States of such dishonor? Now Python threatens to sue me. Me, mind you, and I already out a thousand dollars."

"Sue you for what?"

"Publicly impugning his honor."

"Such sensitivity. Look, Fowler, it was ten a.m. last Friday that you talked over plans for the diary with father, eh?" The agent nodded. "At eleven he was back at his club, at twelve he was at the Mulvany where he stayed until a few minutes before he brought the diary to you, all approximate hours, but close. I doubt if there's time in there for him to have gone to Python, don't you?"

"Where then did Python get his handout?"

"I don't know for sure, but I'll say this, Fowler, a little promiscuity in a family goes further than all its virtues."

"A little!" Fowler cried. "You had better read the diary."

"I intend to—if I may have it now."

Fowler took a key from a ring in his pocket and opened the bottom drawer to a filing cabinet. He gave the red leather-bound book into Jimmie's hands. "If ever. . . ."

"If ever," Jimmie interrupted him. He lifted the book to his nose. "Smells like iodine, doesn't it—old ink?"

"That's what it is!" Fowler cried. "The old reprobate wrote it himself!"

"I didn't say that's what it is," Jimmie said irritably. "I said old ink smells like iodine."

Fowler opened his mouth to say he didn't say Jimmie said . . . and then decided to let it go. He went to the door with Jimmie. "Will you shake hands, at least, Mr. Jarvis?"

"I don't know why I should. I have a very considerable pride in my father."

"You ought to," Fowler said. "He was the most charming rogue I've ever met."

"When the estate is settled," Jimmie said, "I shall see that you get the thousand back."

38

Jimmie drove directly to party headquarters. Mike Zabriski intercepted him. "Hey, young fella, what are you going to do about the item in the Python's column?"

"You'll have my answer by tonight, Mike. In fact, the whole damn town will have it."

"That's more like my boy," Mike said, and clapped him on the back. A cloud of cigar smoke pursued Jimmie to the inner office door. When Mike was happy he blew his smoke in clouds. In temper, he blew smoke rings, enough of them to strangle a man.

But not around Jimmie Jarvis, no sir. Jimmie thought, and roused Madeline Barker from her punctuation of the

convention keynote address. "Read this for me, Jimmie.
See if you get enough breath in the right places."

"Right now I'm saving my breath for the right places,"
Jimmie said. "And I want you to come with me."

Madeline looked up.

"How would you like to introduce me to Lemuel
Python?"

"I'd be delighted," she said. "Preferably by cablegram.
When?"

Jimmie looked at his watch. "When he gets up this
morning."

Miss Barker took her purse from the drawer. "Before he
goes to bed. He sleeps from eleven till seven, a.m. into
p.m. that is."

They intercepted the columnist leaving his office, and
Madeline introduced Jimmie.

"He's a Boy Scout," the columnist said, looking Jimmie
over while he scratched his ribs with his thumbnail. Jimmie
waited, letting his tongue play over the edge of his teeth.
The columnist grinned. "Who was it said 'the righteous are
bold?' "

"Nedda Bopper," Jimmie said. "You've got something
that belongs to me. I want it."

"Come into the Pit," Python said, and led the way back
into his office. The walls were covered with celebrities'
pictures, all signed with love, admiration, and abiding faith.
A solid mile of hollow teeth, Jimmie thought.

"I've come for my briefcase," he said. "My father
borrowed it . . . and laid it down."

"Where?"

Jimmie took a long chance, met Python's eyes squarely,
and answered what he surmised might have been the truth:
"Where by the Grace of God, he wasn't found dead."

"Okay, Boy Scout," Python said. "I've been waiting for
you to pick it up."

"When did she give it to you?" Jimmie tried another
guess.

This one was a failure. "*She* didn't give it to me, so stop
fishing. I don't even know *she*, except as somebody you just
introduced into the conversation." Python opened the

middle drawer of his desk and took out the initialed dispatch case. He threw it down on the desk in front of Jimmie. "Let's just say I found it."

"Do you always publish ads in your column like that one?" Jimmie said.

Python pushed his hat back on his head. "Did you expect me to clear that one with Madeline?"

"You know, there just might have been some wisdom in that," Jimmie said. He opened the briefcase and checked the notes within it—the General's samples of the diary. He merely glanced at one sheet. "Shall we go?"

Python again snapped the lock on his office door. The hall was crowded with people. At the other side of the elevators was the city editor's office, almost as crowded as Herald Square.

"Yes, sir," Jimmie said as the elevator braked for their floor. "That would have been a wise precaution to take in this case. You see these are my father's notes for a bit of fiction he was writing based on something that might have happened about a hundred years ago."

Python put his hands on his hips, and looked from Madeline to Jimmie, to Madeline, to Jimmie. "Who the hell do you think you're kidding, Boy Scout?"

"It's the truth, Lem," Madeline said.

"Oh, so now it's the truth," the columnist sneered. "He sat out the war in England," Python jerked his thumb at Jimmie, "rendezvousing with this Lady wha'sher-name, and now you try to tell me those intimate tid-bits happened a hundred years ago? Oh, sister!"

Miss Barker flung around to Jimmie. "Jimmie, I did not confirm or deny it. I left that for you to answer."

"Thank you," Jimmie said. "And here's my answer."

As the elevator door opened, he brought his fist up with the drive of a hammer, and catching Python under the chin, he lifted him into the emerging passengers, all of them staggering back into the elevator. "Like we Boy Scouts always say, Python, 'Be Prepared!'" He pushed through the crowd then and walked downstairs. Madeline Barker needed to skip to catch up with him.

"I think that should be adequate for Python, the Party, and possibly you, my dear," Jimmie said.

"It was a masterful blow," she said adoringly.

And sure enough, even Python's journal gave the incident the afternoon headline: JARVIS DEFENDS HONOR, THRASHES PYTHON.

Miss Barker concocted a lovely story for the reporters, and Jimmie could not be reached for comment.

39

Mrs. Norris arrived back at Mrs. Joyce's from Brooklyn mid-afternoon in a state of some bewilderment. There had been times when Mag seemed her old sour self whose company was pleasure only when you knew she best enjoyed herself in that disposition. Then again, Mag had perked up and talked about the trip she and Mr. Robinson were going to take soon—perhaps to Scotland. "But there," she ended up, "he's only talking to cheer me up. He hasn't even the time to come up and see you in Nyack."

Nor the inclination, Mrs. Norris had thought. The best she had come back from Brooklyn with was Mag's promise to persuade Mr. Robinson that she should spend a week with Annie in Nyack whether he wanted to come or not.

Mrs. Norris stood outside Helene's door for a moment listening to the sound of the chisel on stone. She hated to interrupt anyone at work but especially Mrs. Joyce whose power to make a stone look mortal was awesome indeed. But at that moment Jimmie came whistling up the street. He had his own key, the propriety of which Mrs. Norris refused to think on for the moment.

Then he held it under her nose. "This is a day key, Mrs. Norris, not a night key."

She drew herself up to her best height. "Such a thought never crossed the threshold of my mind, Master Jamie."

"Then it was wiping its feet at the door," he said.

Between them they had the tea brewed when Helene came out of her workroom. "You two are in high spirits," she said.

"Did you see the afternoon paper?" said Jimmie. "I just happen to have one in my pocket."

Jasper Tully arrived soon thereafter with a second copy. He also carried the General's valise, surrendered to him by the property clerk. The final report was in from the Medical Examiner—General Jarvis had died of coronary thrombosis. Tully was glad to hear Jimmie had had a good day, his own having been a misery. Furthermore, the D.A. was wondering why, as long as he seemed to be running on Jimmie's ticket for Lieutenant Governor, he didn't resign from the District Attorney's staff.

"Not a bad idea, Tully for Lieutenant Governor," Jimmie said. He wiped butter from his fingers. "Well, shall we have a look at father's masterpiece? By the way, just for the hell of it, I stopped by an expert's. It was his opinion this was genuine, so let it not be said that the old boy did a sloppy job of forgery."

"Forgery?" Mrs. Norris put her fist to her breast.

"Oh, without a doubt," Jimmie said. "I have no doubt he was working on it all afternoon of the day he died."

Mr. Tully lifted the book to his nose. "Is it written in iodine?"

"No, it's ink all right. He had the formula for the ink made in those days, and a sample of the shade he wanted all in my dispatch case. I suppose in time we'll turn up the chemist who prepared it for him, or the printer. Chemist, I suppose."

Mrs. Norris lifted her chin at the word printer. Something began to happen inside her, and she had to find a magazine to fan herself.

"When he was experimenting for himself," Tully said, "he must've been using iodine. I found three bottles up there."

Mrs. Norris cleared her throat. "And the gardener brought a fistful of nibs in from the flower bed under his window."

Helene laughed aloud. "What a marvelous scandal this

might have made!" She had taken the diary from Tully's hands and read a passage.

"You have a charming sense of humor," Jimmie said.

"Oh," she said, "here it is—the passage that landed poor Python in the hospital."

"Read it out!" Tully said.

Mrs. Norris could not share their mirth. She was remembering the talking-to she had given the Nyack telephone office for having billed two calls to Brooklyn instead of one. She just could not listen to the things they were laughing and shaking their heads over. But the good Lord be praised, at least, she had had the wisdom not to make her censure of the old gentleman too loud. Oh, she could remember now the occasions on which Mr. Robinson had been to Nyack. He had been introduced to General Jarvis, and Mr. Robinson was not a man to consider his position in life. She had often thought he didn't know his own place, making free to wander into the garage. Oh, oh, oh. Her head reeled with the chagrin of it.

"Well," Jasper Tully said finally, "there's two men dead, and while there's a thing or two explained, we're not much closer to the how, why and who of that." He accounted then his own day, starting with his last visit in Brooklyn. "One thing kind of significant to me about The Rock's banking habits, Jimmie, he made his deposits every other day, and he always got his receipts in duplicate."

"A partner?" Jimmie said.

"I don't see any other explanation," Tully said: "The Brooklyn police say it could be tax information. They got a tracer on that, but I'd go along on the partner idea."

"I suppose we're reasonably safe in assuming that it was not Father," Jimmie said.

"Maybe you are," Tully drawled. "I'm not making any assumptions from here on in. I've put out a questionnaire to every bank in Brooklyn, Manhattan, Queens and the Bronx. I want to know if anybody else in New York was in the habit of making deposits on alternate days. The Rock's business practices sound to me like a crook's check on a crook."

Jimmie grinned, catching some of Tully's slow fire. It had been a long time since they worked together, and he had all but forgotten the strain tightening with each new discovery, the agony of each frustration. Tully gave the impression of being a man of infinite patience, but if you knew him like Jimmie did, you could see the fire kindling.

"What else, Jasp?"

Tully shrugged. "I went to see a thug called Slim, The Rock's personal servant, the guy who wasn't with him when he got taken for the last mile."

"Did you ask him why not, where he was?"

"Nope. That's the Brooklyn boys' work. And you can't ask a man about where he wasn't. Only where he was. Anyway I was hoping to tie up the General's fair lady with The Rock. It didn't work out. No women in The Rock's life at all. No women, no liquor . . . only horses and foreign sports cars, and he wouldn't talk about the horses."

"The cars he had in common with father," Jimmie said.

Tully nodded. "Do you know that Austin-Healey of The Rock's is an exact replica of one owned by the Duke of Glower?"

"So?" said Jimmie.

Tully sighed. "I was hoping that might mean something to you."

"How did he know they were alike?" Jimmie said, trying to oblige.

"Knew somebody who was an expert—according to Slim. Just seems funny, being an expert on something like that, and the friend of a gangster."

"Let me tell you something, Jasper, rum-running in its day made an aristocracy among gangdom. Johnny The Rock was the last Mogul. There were morning coats at his funeral."

"I should've gone myself," Tully said. "That may turn out to be the biggest mistake I made on this case, not being there to look over the chauffeurs."

Jimmie slapped him on the back. "You can't be two places at once, Jasp."

"Funny," Tully said, lifting his sad eyes from their contemplation of his own shoetops, "you never said that when you were District Attorney." He gathered his feet under him. "If I get a wire recorder down here, would you be willing to go over it from the beginning tonight?"

"Willing, but not eager," Jimmie said, thinking it must start at Albany for him.

"Mrs. Norris?"

"Aye." She thought of the day the old man asked her for a few dollars until the first of the month. He had gone straight from her refusal to the family papers in the attic.

"Do you mind, Mrs. Joyce?"

Helene shook her head, and thought of seeing in Lem Python's column that Madeline Barker was lunching with James Ransom Jarvis.

"I guess for me it starts on Water Street," Tully said, "me as a stranger trying to place a bet at the one-armed restaurant called Minnie's before we staked it out." He pointed to the diary in Jimmie's hand. "What are you going to do with that?"

"Put it right back in the attic—and if it shows up a hundred years hence, let them worry about its authenticity. A little scandal then may save the Jarvis name from oblivion."

"You sound just like your father," Mrs. Norris said with vast disapproval.

40

Mrs. Norris told no one where she was going in the morning. Mr. James was near ruin for the public discussion of his private family affairs. If there was matter for disgrace in her own family, Mrs. Norris intended to keep it to herself as long as possible. She took the subway, a bus and a taxi, and then went by shank's mare, the last block to Mr. Robinson's printing shop.

It was a cold and windy day, and having got her courage to its highest point for the encounter, she was furious to find the place locked up as tight as a bailiff's fist. She pounded on the doors, front and back, and then seriously contem-

plated breaking a window. The prospect of being caught at
it restrained her. She crossed from the back way to a
lunchroom where she hoped for a cup of hot tea to tune up
her powers of cogitation. Just as she was going into the
foggy-windowed restaurant, Minnie's, she remembered that
this was the place which Mr. Tully had been watching the
night he saw the General go by at top speed.

Mrs. Norris sat on the last stool, near the cash register.
Two other customers were huddled over steaming cups at
the other end of the counter. Minnie came to her, drying his
hands on his apron. Though she loathed coffee, she ordered
it, thinking that asking for tea might antagonize the
restaurant keeper, and that she did not want to do. He was
pleasant enough to give her courage. She remembered that
Mr. Tully had tried unsuccessfully to place a bet here.

"I'm a great follower of the horses," she said, when
Minnie brought her coffee, "or I was in the old country. A
friend of mine down the street said you might put me next to
where I could lay a few dollars on a nag."

Minnie looked at her through half-closed eyes. "Who's
your friend?"

"His name's Jim. He works for the coal yard at the
corner," she said with a fine glibness.

"Jim," Minnie repeated. "Have a doughnut with your
coffee." He brought one and gave it to her without her
saying please, no, or thank you. Meanwhile he was
examining her from all angles. He turned on the radio then,
loud enough so that the two men at the other end of the
counter needed to raise their voices to talk to one another.
He took a dime from the cash register and went into the
phone booth behind her. A telephone stood unused beside
the register.

Mrs. Norris could feel the pickup of her heartbeat. She
was glad the two working men were present at the other end
of the counter.

Minnie came out, turned down the radio, and gave her a
wink and a nod of his head. Whether to be glad or sad, Mrs.
Norris didn't know. If he took her money no doubt the
information would be valuable to Mr. Tully . . . but she

couldn't even name a horse. Worse, she couldn't name the park where they were running.

The two working men got up, paid their bill at the cash register and left.

"More coffee?" Minnie asked her.

She was already nauseous with what she had had. She shook her head. "Could I look at your paper?" she said.

"Why not?" Minnie handed her the *News*.

She tried not to make obvious haste in finding the sports page. With the rattle of pages, however, she did not hear the man come up behind her. She jumped when he spoke.

"This the lady?"

Since there was no other present, it was an unnecessary question, but Mrs. Norris spun around, and managed to get her toes on the floor. It was the round-faced chauffeur. He caught her arm and helped her rather roughly off the stool. "I ain't got much time, lady, but I want to take you on a little trip."

"No thank you," Mrs. Norris said, trying to jerk her arm free.

"It won't hurt a bit," he said.

"I haven't paid for my coffee," Mrs. Norris cried, already being borne through the door.

"It's on the house," Minnie called after them. "Tell the D.A. to come around in his own pants next time."

Foolish, foolish me, Mrs. Norris thought. Before her was a spotless black limousine. Surely not . . .

"Hold on there, man!"

Mrs. Norris was almost as happy as of old to see Mr. Robinson then.

"This is my sister-in-law," he said, "who the devil are you?"

The burly one stood staring, "Nick said. . . ."

"Get away out of here and leave this woman alone!" Mr. Robinson began waving his arms as though he were scattering chickens.

Mrs. Norris jerked her arm free of the big one's hand. He had not much of a grasp on her. For all Mr. Robinson's act they were no strangers, these two, and that was the most frightening thing of all.

Mr. Robinson took her in charge. He began to walk her across the street. "Were you on your way to see me, Annie? You shouldn't speak to strangers in this neighborhood, you know."

She was by no means sure she should speak to as intimate an acquaintance as her brother-in-law, for that matter. But she had undertaken to pilot this mission herself, and it was now under full sail.

Mr. Robinson took her through the plant, all the machinery covered and still, and in his private office sat her down in a leather chair. "Now, my dear, tell me what happened."

Mrs. Norris decided on a direct question. "Mr. Robinson, did you help General Jarvis with that forgery he tried to sell as a diary?"

Robbie threw back his head and laughed. "Discovered so soon!" he cried. "I wonder if he wouldn't have carried it off if he had lived. He was a remarkable man, Annie . . . Yes, I helped him. And proud I was to be asked, if you want to know."

"I see," said Mrs. Norris, not prepared for so frank an admission. "Who was the man you just took me out of the clutches of?"

Mr. Robinson had no intention of being frank in that matter. "I have no notion, having but seen him around the neighborhood, Annie. I suspect he's a gangster, if you must know. That's why I came up on the run. He may have mistook you for someone else. Or were you up to something suspicious?"

Oh, the wily one, she thought. If she admitted now trying to place the bet, he would be off the hook and away. Bad as she was at it, she must try a little acting of her own. She picked up a magazine and fanned herself. "A gangster did you say, Mr. Robinson? Do you think he was planning to give me a ride in that, that hearse?"

"That seemed your direction when I rescued you."

She fanned herself more violently. "Do you have a drop of whiskey, Mr. Robinson? My heart's palpitating near to bursting."

Mr. Robinson swung open a cabinet door in the midst of

his books, and took a bottle out and with it a glass. Mrs. Norris got another start. The paneling was covered with pictures of foreign cars . . . The Duke of Glower, she thought, Rocco The Rock and the Duke of Glower. Her brother-in-law poured her a drink, his face set in a hard little smile of toleration. Whether or not she was fooling him, she didn't know. Likely not. But it served his purpose to play the game with her.

"Mr. Robinson, I'll need a drop of water to run that down in. When it's my heart, I cannot take it neat."

Robbie bowed and went out of the office with a glass.

She hopped to the opened panel, for opposite the liquor cabinet was its match, another cabinet, and she prayed it might open on the same key. It did. There was a boxful of money within it, and a neat little bundle of bank deposit slips. One of them she managed to loose and pocket. She locked the cabinet and put the key where she had found it. On the wall of the panel was taped a card with a phone number: EX 4–1587. She had just managed to fling herself back in the chair when Mr. Robinson returned. If he knew she had been out of it, he did not let on.

"I'm taking Mag to Florida, by the way, Annie. I've sold the business here, which is why everything is shut up."

"Florida?" she repeated. Remembering then her need for it, she sipped the water and downed the whiskey.

"It's a fine place for Mag. The Brooklyn climate is bad for her health, the doctors say."

"She was hoping it was Scotland you'd take her to, Mr. Robinson. That's what I came to talk to you about."

"Is it—and not the old gentleman's forgeries?"

"Oh, them," she said. "They'll soon be forgot."

"As will we all when we are gone, Annie. Scotland would kill her . . . as Florida may me. Now I have work to do. Can I put you in a taxi for somewhere? They're hard to find in this neighborhood, taxis."

"I wish you would," she said. "I'd prefer not to meet the gentleman with the limousine again."

Half-fact, half-fantasy, Mrs. Norris thought, once more walking out into God's sunlight. At the end of the block, Mr. Robinson hailed a cab. It was occupied, but the driver called out to wait. He would be right back.

"I don't suppose you have time to stop and see Mag?" Mr. Robinson said, at the cab door.

"I'm in a bit of a hurry to get back to Manhattan," Mrs. Norris said.

Robinson grinned. "I'll bet you are. Good-bye, Annie."

Mrs. Norris did not know what sort of impression she had left with her brother-in-law. All that money . . . and the deposit slips. She took it out of her purse and looked at it. The First Federal Bank. That was the bank in front of which the gangster Rocco had been picked up for his last ride. There was no doubt at all that it was Robbie who was getting the duplicate deposit slips. Poor Mag. Poor herself, having to confess this in the family. She leaned forward and asked the cabbie to stop at the first public phone and wait while she made a call.

She dialed EX 4–1587. Presently a man answered.

"Who is this?" Mrs. Norris tried to be authoritative.

"You got the wrong number, lady. This is a unlisted phone." Whoever it was hung up. Not a cultured voice certainly.

Mrs. Norris put in a call to the Manhattan District Attorney's office and asked for Jasper Tully. He was expected in soon. Not soon enough for Mrs. Norris. "I want to leave him a message then. It's very important. This is Mrs. Norris, Mrs. Annie Norris."

"What number are you calling from, Mrs. Norris?"

She gave the number. "But I won't be here! It's a public phone. Now I want you to tell Mr. Tully—I have one of the other bank deposit slips, one of the duplicates. Do you have that?"

"Yes, ma'am." It was the District Attorney's secretary, and she sounded competent as she repeated the message.

"And I want you to give him this number to trace—it's unlisted and it may be important."

The woman took the number and repeated it. "Anything else, Mrs. Norris?"

"I should think that's enough," Mrs. Norris said, and hung up.

She had something else on her own mind, however, something the goonish chauffeur had said that she did not want to forget. It had an odd but persistent association in her mind with something she had seen or heard recently.

She returned to the cab and promised the driver an extra dollar for speed.

The cabbie squinted at her in the mirror as they pulled away from the curb, "If you mean I got to stay ahead of that black limousine, lady, I ain't making rash promises."

Mrs. Norris twisted around and peered out the rear window. Loyal as a shadow, the great black car kept pace with them. She leaned forward in the seat then and raised her voice. "We'll have worse than a rash you and me, young man, I promise, if you don't keep ahead of it."

But the limousine narrowed the distance between the cars as soon as the cabbie stretched it.

41

Jasper Tully was giving himself an hour off the top of every day now to try and find the General's fair lady. He had that very morning located his third parakeet within the Eldorado exchange and within two blocks of the florist shop, and he had listened to the laments of many a sad and lonely woman any one of whom would have been glad to open her door to the General, he thought. But he was reasonably sure that none he had talked to so far had.

Calling in to his office, he picked up Mrs. Norris' message. Acting on her own—and this was the reason she had been in the D.A.'s office as long as Tully himself—the secretary had ordered tracers on Ex 4–1587 as well as the phone from which Mrs. Norris had called.

"Mr. Tully, the unlisted phone belonged to John Rocco."

"Where the devil did she get it?" Tully cried. And then answered himself. "Never mind. Where did she call from?"

The woman gave him the exact location, and Mrs.

Norris' word that she would not be there. Tully swore under
his breath. Not only had she taken upon herself to do police
work, by the looks of things, but she was expecting him to
sit and wait for her to get in touch with him again.

He called Jimmie at his office. Jimmie's first reaction was
alarm. But Mrs. Norris was a sensible woman, he assured
Tully.

"All right then," Tully said, "she can sit in my office or
wherever she lands and sensibly wait for us. Just in case
something went wrong over there, I'm going over."

"Pick me up on your way," Jimmie said. "I'll wait in
front of the building."

The public phone from which Mrs. Norris called was in a
cigar store just three blocks from Minnie's Restaurant on
Water Street. The man behind the counter swore no woman
had been in his place that morning, either to phone or buy
tobacco. Obviously, one had. The D.A.'s secretary did not
make up the phone number nor the address. Tully and
Jimmie went on to the restaurant. Minnie gave them a cold
stare, and the surly retort: "I don't serve no women in this
place."

Tully called his office. No word yet.

Jimmie called Helene, also from Minnie's phone booth.
The line was busy. He sat, the door of the booth open,
waiting and thinking. She had relatives, a sister in Brooklyn, and she was worried about her.

"Jasp, didn't you bring her over to Brooklyn yesterday?
Do you remember the name of her sister?"

Tully was staring out the window, through the streaks of
steam. He was reminded of rainy days in his childhood, his
nose against the parlor window. "Robinson," he said, and
even as he said it, he saw the name printed in white letters
on the brick wall across the way. He turned his head quick
enough to suspect Minnie of having listened with very large
ears. Minnie smiled at him. That was enough to make a
more gullible man than Tully suspicious.

"Come on, Jimmie."

They strode across the street. With no response at the
back door, they tried the front, also without results. Tully
had a feeling about the place, the minute they had circled it

and he peered in the front of the building. The two benches, the great ashstands, the string of faded lettering samples in the window told of a very poor business—in printing.

"How do we get in?" said Jimmie, having much the same feeling.

Tully gave the matter but an instant's thought. "I smell smoke," he said, and Jimmie could not be sure whether it was a ruse or reality. Tully put the butt of his revolver through the glass of the door window. As soon as he could do it without destroying himself he hoisted his body up and in. He picked up the nearest phone, got the precinct police, identified himself, and told them he had broken in at this address, thinking there was a fire in the building. A mistake. Sorry.

He and Jimmie stayed just long enough to confirm their first suspicions. Minnie was a duck all right, a sitting duck, a decoy. This was the real thing, a bookie's paradise. Or had been. The shop was closed. All the phones save one were dead. Disconnected. Tully consulted the phone book. Having delivered Mrs. Norris to the corner, he was able to find Robinson's home address quickly.

He called the Brooklyn D.A.'s office to get out the warrant for Robinson and to get a squad car out here to go over the print shop. He opened up the siren on the way to the Robinson residence. It had been two hours and ten minutes since Mrs. Norris had called in, and she had not been heard from since.

42

Mrs. Norris was far too busy with her own pursuits to think of calling anyone. Her cab had parted company with the limousine at the entrance to the tunnel. She credited her driver for it and gave herself up to thought of her sister. In all these years Mag had boasted the good provider, she had never questioned the whence of providence. She would soon be on her way to Florida now thinking the state itself designed for her comfort.

She went up the steps to Mrs. Joyce's thinking not for an instant of the four dollars and fifty cent fare she had paid. Helene opened the door almost as soon as she rang. A sweet woman.

"Mrs. Joyce, do you remember the General's valise Mr. Tully brought last night?"

It sat where Tully had put it down in the living room, undisturbed by the cleaning woman. Someone had taken the trouble to lock it, however, and the devil knew what he had done with the key. With a cuticle scissors and an eyebrow tweezers, they managed to open it.

"It may be my imagination," Mrs. Norris said, spreading one of the newspapers on the floor. She was on her knees like a child with the comics. Helene spread the other paper. "I remember it, flitting in and out the corner of my eye . . . Nick, Nick, Nick . . . the name Nick. The big, moon-faced one, when he tried to get me into his limousine this morning . . . Nick, he said. I heard it. . . ."

Helene but glanced at her, an instant's admiration. She was traveling like a tumbleweed in the wind Mrs. Norris blew up. "Here it is, here it is!" she cried, and read aloud the account of Nick Casey's arrest as a Peeping Tom . . .

"Read on, read on, girl!"

"'. . . Casey was released on the sworn testimony of Miss Flora Tims that. . . .'"

"That's the one!" Mrs. Norris cried. "Flora! 'Blossoms for my blossom'. That idiot of a florist! Flowers for my Flora, of course! Do they give her address?"

"'Miss Flora Tims of 763 East Fifty-ninth,'" Helene read.

"Would you be willing to confront her with me, Mrs. Joyce?"

"I'd be delighted to meet her," Helene said. "Though she may not be nearly so eager to meet us, Mrs. Norris."

Mrs. Norris grunted, getting up from her knees. "We'll be very hospitable," she said. She folded the paper and tore the Casey item from it. "Let's go."

43

"You can pound all day on that door, mister. They all left about a hour ago. Florida, I hear. Driving in a lovely black car, this long . . ." The woman stretched her hands as though she were playing a squeeze-box.

"All," said Tully. "How many?"

"Well, there was the chauffeur. Mind you, the Robinsons with a chauffeur, and him coming over a immigrant without the nails to scratch himself. . . ."

"Besides the chauffeur?" Jimmie interrupted.

"Mr. and Mrs. Robinson. They're Scotch you know . . ."

"Anybody else?"

"A big man, handsome. Lots of authority. I bet he's a magnet."

"I'll bet," said Jimmie, "Did you notice the license?"

The woman slowly put her own construction to that question. "Should I of?"

"Only if you thought it was unusual." Tully took over easily.

"Oh, it was unusual enough, but Mr. Robinson, he's got a regular menagerie of friends, coming in and going out at all hours the last few days."

Jimmie and the detective exchanged glances. Obviously, Mr. Robinson had been making book from home in the last few days, or as much of the old trade as he could manage from a residential address. Everything had been in a state of flux since the night The Rock was murdered.

"I'll come back and see you some day, ma'am," Tully said and tipped his hat.

Jimmie followed him back to the car. At the first police call box the detective stopped. He asked that a two state alarm be put out to intercept the limousine heading for Florida.

157

44

" 'Two and a half room apartments,' " Mrs. Norris read as she and Helene crossed the street. "I've often wondered what a half-room was, and what they did with the other half they didn't rent you in these places." She found herself chattering and paying precious little attention to what she was saying. She would not have said she was nervous, but she found herself very, very grateful that Helene Joyce was with her. She caught Mrs. Joyce's hand as she found the name TIMS on the box. The hand was cold and damp, but firm, telling her she was not alone in fear or fierceness.

Helene rang a bell other than Miss Tims'. The buzzer sounded to let them in. "This way if she's in we'll be face to face with her at least when she slams the door on our foot."

"Clever, very clever," Mrs. Norris said.

"Our foot," Helene repeated, as she and Mrs. Norris squeezed into the elevator, and giggled.

"This was made for love not elevation," Mrs. Norris cracked, as they grindingly got off the first floor.

Outside Miss Tims' door the two women stood and looked at each other. Then Mrs. Norris gave the bell a push. Within the apartment the parakeet started a racket. It carried on for a moment, then stopped like a machine turned off. Mrs. Norris thought of a remark but her mouth was suddenly dry.

The little eye-view door opened. "Why don't you ring downstairs and give a girl warnin'?"

Mrs. Norris lifted her chin. "Miss Tims, I am the late General Jarvis's housekeeper." That, she calculated, would either get them in or get them out in a hurry.

Miss Tims unlatched her door without a word, opened it, and stood before them in her slip. "Wouldn't you like to come in, Mrs. Norris? I'm awful glad to make your acquaintance."

"This is Mrs. Joyce."

Miss Tims began to sniffle, and nothing could have made Mrs. Norris feel less at ease. She had been prepared to beat this woman over the head if necessary, but certainly not to console her. Maybe with her clothes on she looked like a flapper, but this way she looked like something out of an old English movie.

Meanwhile the parakeet was squawking a noise that sounded very much like "Take it off, take it off," wherever he was.

Miss Tims lifted a sheet from over the cage.

"Ramsom? Ramsom?" said the bird.

Mrs. Norris was distinctly embarrassed. "He talks very nicely," she said.

Miss Tims then burst into sobs. "Oh, Mrs. Norris, it was just a terrible mistake, him being jealous of Nick. It mightn't ever've happened if it wasn't for that."

Helene took a well-cologned handkerchief from her purse and gave it to Flora.

Flora dabbed her eyes with it and then breathed the smell of it into her lungs. "Gee, honey, this smells real sweet. What is it?"

"Peasblossom," Helene said. "You may keep it."

"Thanks just awfully. Ransom used to bring me essences from all over the world. . . . poor dear. I miss him so."

"About him and Nick," Mrs. Norris prompted. It gave her a most uncanny feeling to speak familiarly of a gangster. She had better get used to it, having one in the family. God's righteousness smiting her for her pride.

"It was all a mistake, don't you see?"

"Not quite," she said.

Flora bit her lip. "I'll show it to you, but don't you tell anybody I got it, 'specially Nick."

" 'Specially Nick," Mrs. Norris promised willingly.

The girl went into the bedroom, the stupid bird calling after her "Night-night, night-night." In a moment she returned and handed to Mrs. Norris the note which had first sent the General into a rage when he received it in Robbie's office. Helene read it over her shoulder.

I want a piece of your little plum. Make arrangements
while you are there tonight or I will make them for you.
You are an old man. There is enough for both of us.

                                                Nick Casey

"He thought I was the little plum, don't you see?"

Mrs. Norris nodded. At least she could see that Nick
Casey was the link in the chain that had brought the General
low. "And it wasn't you?"

"I hadn't seen Nick for years till then. And Nick was
talkin' about a business deal he wanted in on—out in some
silly place in Brooklyn." Flora laid a finger as limp as her
backbone on Mrs. Norris' arm. "Furthermore, I don't know
what Ransom was doin' out there at all. The note wasn't
meant for him in the first place. It was meant for somebody
else entirely."

"Mr. Rocco?" said Mrs. Norris.

"Sh-sh," Flora said. "He's dead."

"So is the General," Mrs. Norris snapped.

"But he died different," Flora wailed.

"That is an understatement of some proportions,"
Helene remarked. She had the note from Mrs. Norris' hand,
and was about to put it in her purse. Flora's eyes were not
too wet to see it. She rubbed her fingers together, the
gesture of "hand-it-over." It had been worth a try, at least,
Helene thought.

"A girl's got to have some protection," Flora said, naive
as a fox. "You ought to know all about that, honey. This is
my insurance policy." On her way to the bedroom again,
she paused. "I don't suppose Ransom left me anything?
I've been dyin' to find out only Nick wouldn't let me. And I
don't care about money. I just want to know if he mentioned
me."

Suddenly there was a long ring and a short at the
doorbell. The parakeet began to screetch "Ransom, Ran-
son," and Flora leapt for the bird's coverlet. "That's Nick
downstairs now, I promised him to go to Florida with him
and I don't want to go, I don't want to go away from here
ever . . . Ransom and I was so happy."

"Miss Tims, I should prefer not to meet Mr. Casey

here," Mrs. Norris said. Helene was already looking out the window.

"Not out there in daylight, honey," Flora cried. "Nick'd look there first if he was lookin'.' I got to hide this note. Why don't you two just roll under the beds? There's two of them, one for each of you . . ."

Since the choice of escapeways was even narrower, the two women looked at each other and then abandoned their dignity.

45

The detective and Jimmie were caught between wrath and despair arriving at Mrs. Joyce's house and finding her gone as well. This was the logical place for Mrs. Norris to have come—unless she had found out far more than her phone call intimated. Tully went to the kitchen, Jimmie into the living room to see if there was a note anywhere. There Jimmie found the General's valise gaping, one of the pages of the newspaper on the floor, spread open. He called out to Tully, and before the detective reached him he had found the other paper, one item having been torn from it.

It took Jasper Tully nine minutes on the phone with the newspaper's librarian.

"Nick Casey! That's it all right. . . ." He listened to the rest of the story, shaking his head at his own blindness. Even while he listened, his eyes wandered through the story of the St. Patrick's Day preparations. . . . the perfect decoy. Just like Minnie's restaurant.

He wrote the name and address of Miss Flora Tims, thanked the librarian and hung up. "Blossoms for my little blossom," he muttered in disgust. "Do you know what's wrong with the world, Jimmie?" He waved his arms in the air. "Too many distractions! Nobody pays attention! Nobody listens. Everybody talks. That's what hell is going to be like when we get there."

"Maybe that's where we are now," Jimmie said. "Are we on our way?"

"With the throttle open."

46

Mrs. Norris at least had had the presence of mind to go under feet first, as it were, so that her head was beneath the foot of the bed, and she could plainly hear all that went on in the livingroom. Mr. Casey was in an ugly mood. Mrs. Norris could see his feet and Flora's, toes to toes, suddenly Flora's were lifted from the floor entirely, and it was not because she was caught in a loving embrace.

"Make up your mind, baby. You're going with me in five minutes whether it's with a suitcase or in it." The man's pointed toes were suddenly flapping across the bedroom. In its cage, cover or no, the parakeet was screaming with glee. Casey flung Miss Tims on the bed, fortunately the one under which was Helene. There wasn't room for an ounce of play between Mrs. Norris and the springs. Casey opened the closet door, helping himself to clothes and suitcase, which he tossed onto Mrs. Norris' bed. "Now you get them packed pronto. I'm going to take care of that bird."

That would be a mercy, Mrs. Norris thought.

Flora began to scream and thump the bed. "I won't go and you leave my bird alone! Ransom bought him for me at Christmas."

"I'll buy ya a peacock for the Fourth of July!" Casey shouted.

"I just want you to go away and leave me alone," Flora wailed.

"Un-unh. You know too much about Nick, baby. And Nick don't like to see you gettin' lonesome."

He stomped out then, and there was a terrible flurry and threshing about in the living room. Flora lifted the skirt of the bedspread, throwing some light on Mrs. Norris. "Can't you help me save my poor little bird? I'm goin' to tell him you're here if you don't."

Nick roared from the bedroom door: "The goddamn bird flew out the window! He'll be blabbin' up and down the neighborhood, "Ransom, Ransom, Ransom.""

"He'll get pneumonia out in this weather!" Flora screamed and ran to the window.

"I'm losing patience, baby," Nick said.

"Nickie—I don't know a thing about you, exceptin' that note Ransom got from you by mistake . . ."

"Keep talkin'."

"If I was to give that to you now, would you go along to Florida, and jus' forget ever meetin' up with me again?"

"I'd love to forget it, baby."

"Swear it?"

"My word as a gentleman," Casey said.

The sound of Flora's heels clacked across the floor.

"Thanks," Casey said after a moment, and Mrs. Norris could hear the tearing of paper.

There was a long ring and a short at the door. "That's Echo," Casey said. "I'm gonna wait in the car, baby. He'll help you pack. Come here now! You ain't going out any window when my back is turned." Casey must have been hauling her by the arm for her feet stumbled after his to the door.

"But you promised," Flora cried, "you gave me your word!"

"As a gentleman," said Nick. "You know better than that."

"Mrs. Norris?" Helene squeaked.

Mrs. Norris lifted the spread to peer out at her.

"What will we do?" Mrs. Joyce queried in a whisper.

"I wish we could fly out like the bird," she said.

Casey and Flora returned, and with them a man the toes of whose very shoes rose from the floor like black moons, Mrs. Norris thought.

"Now listen to me, baby, and listen good. We got a nice

large trunk on the back of the car. You can go in that—or you can go inside the car sitting beside me like a doll."

Flora's response was to sink into a dead faint, her face six inches away from Mrs. Norris'.

"Bring her any way you can," Casey snarled. "And don't wait to clean up."

"Echo," merely grunted.

Mrs. Norris tensed her fists. She waited, holding her breath until she heard the door close behind Casey. The thing called "Echo" came between the two beds to begin his work on Flora. As though by signal, Mrs. Norris and Helene each grabbed him by a leg, except that Mrs. Norris couldn't hold hers when he began to tumble. She humped out from beneath the bed like a snail, however, and while the thug was twisting and scratching at Helene's grip on his ankle, Mrs. Norris climbed onto the bed and bounded from there upon his back. Helene scrambled out and to her feet.

"Throw water on her, we may need her," Mrs. Norris directed Helene, riding the goon piggy-back while he balked round the room like a mule.

Helene grabbed the only water nearby, a vase with the last of the late General's roses, and dumped it flowers and all on Miss Flora Tims. She rose up in a wrath and Mrs. Norris let go of her hold on "Echo." He went out of the place like a rabbit only a leap and a pant ahead of the vixens.

47

The detective and Jimmie had driven up at the moment "Echo" got out of the limousine to go upstairs. They waited long enough to ascertain that two people were in the car, a man and a woman, and both of them looking like mummies. Then, even as Tully and Jimmie were walking by, the man took his handkerchief from his pocket and wiped his hands.

He pulled himself up in the seat then, using a chrome rail at the side, and from that he wiped the perspiration also. He turned and stared at the building into which the thug had gone.

Tully watched with fascination. Thus was accounted the lack of fingerprints on the door of the General's Jaguar! A mere nervous habit of Mr. Robinson's.

He and Jimmie went into Flora's building, striding quickly, and ringing every bell for entrance into the downstairs hall. They were admitted in time to catch the elevator. The door was closing on the wire cage when Tully recognized Nick Casey. Wherever the gangster had found the stairs he was on his way out of the building. Tully moved with the unexpected speed of a snake, and slithered his lean body out before he was caged in the lift.

Casey caught sight of him then, sprinted across the street and leaped into the driver's seat of the limousine. The car had been parked with the caution of thieves, and it took Casey but an instant to power it on its way. Tully had his revolver in hand. He might have shot out the tires, and again he might have missed. There were bystanders and walkers on the street. Let him go. The alarm was out. He would not go far, even if the license number Tully wrote down was another phony.

The detective moved in the direction from which Casey had come and found the stairs. From some flights up, as he started mounting, someone was starting down pell mell. Then came a shrieking and howling and clamor of heels, all to put him in mind of goats and geese, bats and banshees. He drew his revolver and waited. The moonfaced one came down, his mouth and his eyes like round holes.

Moon-face flung himself against the wall and crumbled there into a heap as the three women hove down upon him. Mrs. Norris was brandishing an ashstand like a shillelah, Mrs. Joyce had a lamp by the neck, and the other one, looking like she'd been washed up in the seaweed, and in her petticoat at that, was waving a fireplace broom.

"All right, ladies. You can turn in your badges," Tully said at the top of his voice. He frisked the blubbering lump at his feet and took from him a snub-nosed revolver and a knife that would have butchered a hog.

Jimmie came down the steps. "Anything I can do?"

"Round up the women," said Tully. "They shouldn't get too fond of this sort of business."

He jerked the goon onto his feet and out to the car. He wanted him to see that Casey had abandoned him. The poor slob stood limp and miserable in bewilderment that the limousine was gone from where he had parked it. The poor slob, Tully thought again, poor bedamned. He was equipped like an arsenal. All Casey ever needed to do was say "sick 'em," and get himself an alibi.

Later, when all the pieces were being fitted together in the D.A.'s office, Tully finished the portrait of "Echo": "A mechanical man, with a kind of a heart, but no brains at all. When it comes to an automobile, there probably isn't a better driver on the road. Nothing else on his mind, don't you see. Absolute concentration. And when he was told to give the note to Johnny Rocco, Casey must have told him no more than was absolutely necessary—a man in his seventies, who drove a sports car, and who could be found at Robbie-the-Printer's."

Mrs. Norris gave a start. "Robbie-the-Printer," she said. "Oh, my goodness."

"He's quite a fellow, your brother-in-law," Mr. Tully said with a wink at Jimmie. "He thinks you might be willing to go bail for him. Says the General told him you had buckets of money."

"Buckets—oh!" Mrs. Norris cried, "well, if he's the good provider Mag still claims he is, he can go bail for himself."

Nick Casey and his passengers had been picked up at the mouth of the Lincoln Tunnel. Mr. Robinson admitted to bookmaking in partnership with Johnny Rocco, but to no other crime. All he had accepted from Mr. Casey was his offer of a ride to Florida after Rocco was killed. As soon as he could then Mr. Robinson had liquidated his assets. And how he had come to know Nick Casey? It took Robbie-the-Printer but a moment to get round that: "He was a friend of a friend . . . of a friend, who was trying to tempt me into another little business on the side . . . the manufacture of famous diaries, you might say."

Mr. Tully had not pursued the question further.

"Whatever's to become of Mag now?" said Mrs. Norris.

"Well, I'll tell you how I see it," Tully said. "Mr. Robinson was inquiring if there was any chance of him being deported. Back to the country of his origin that would be. He would work there at the same trade, legitimate, he says, and he's promised Mag all her life to take her home."

"The canny rogue! A fit companion for the General, excuse me, Master Jamie."

"I was thinking much the same thing," said Jimmie. "You know, Jasp, I have a few friends in the State Department . . ."

"If you want my advice then, my boy," said Tully, "put in a good word quick for a bad egg. I'll press his suit here, if you know what I mean."

The D.A. himself squeezed the confession out of "Echo" and his boss. While Nick was trying to explain to Miss Tims the mistake his boy made that Thursday night, "Echo" returned to Brooklyn to straighten things out there. He arrived back at Robbie-the-Printer's in time to get Johnny Rocco's "No" to Nick's proposition. He trailed him then to the First Federal Bank. He let him get out of the car, make his deposit in the night box, and then took him on the long ride home. By that time Nick was getting out of night court in Manhattan.

Since the District Attorney of two boroughs shared the headlines with "the crusading gubernatorial candidate" on the cracking of the Rocco case and the breakup of the gambling ring in Brooklyn, cooperation flowed like politicos' saliva. At the request of all the ladies involved, their names and the extent of their participation in the roundup were withheld.

By nightfall, the trio of Tully, Norris and Jarvis, started on a last call in the line of duty. Mrs. Joyce said she had had it. She would make dinner for them and kiss them all adieu thereafter. Judge Turner had offered her a fellowship in the peaceful English countryside. Little had she known then how much and how soon she would need it.

48

"Ransom, Ransom, Ransom. . . ." The parakeet was back in his cage.

"Everybody in the neighborhood thought he was callin' them handsome . . . handsome, handsome, handsome. Isn't that cute?"

"Cunning," Jimmie said.

"Miss Tims, we're awful tired, all three of us," Tully said.

"I guess I am, too," she said, "and after you all go I'm goin' to be left all alone again. That's why I took up with Nick. . . ."

"The night General Jarvis died," Tully pushed gently. "Will you tell us what happened after you went to the pawn shop for his medals?"

Miss Tims drew a deep breath and plunged into the story. "Before that, he was so lovin'. I won't ever forget it . . . and he didn't feel very good. We'd had a quarrel you see the night before over Nick. But you know that. And it was so wonderful makin' up and all. And he gave me a hundred dollar bill to get his medals. 'I've got to wear 'em in the morning, Flora. St. Patrick's Day in the morning.' " Flora sniffed back the tears. "When I got home with them he was dead."

"Dead at your house?" Jimmie said.

Flora nodded. "That's how I felt about it too, Mr. Jarvis. I didn't want him disgraced—you know." She shrugged. "I'm nothin' much without him . . . and I knew it would be in the papers. I got a friend down the hall. He works nights sometimes. I gave him fifty dollars and he helped me. We were goin' to pretend that everything was just wonderful. All three of us havin' a wonderful time. And we did it, too. I had to get Nick's chauffer to drive us, but it worked out fine . . . almost."

"Your friend down the hall," Jimmie said, "he's an entertainer?"

Flora nodded.

"A ventriloquist?" Tully prompted.

"How did you know?"

Tully looked at Jimmie. "Dead men don't curse as elegant as it was said your father did that night. And nobody could look him in the face. Rubber legs, the cabbie said. It all fits—now. You didn't waste much time moving him."

"I was afraid of rigor mortis," Flora said.

Tully rubbed the back of his neck. "That must've been the only thing in New York you were afraid of, miss."

"Love finds a way," Flora said calmly.

Mrs. Norris leaned forward. "And did you put his medals on him, dearie?"

"Don't call me 'dearie.' I know what you think I am."

"I saved your life this afternoon, Miss Tims."

"That don't give you the right to call me names. Yes, I put his medals on him. I knew he died proud and I wanted everybody else to know it, too."

"A true Southern lady," Jimmie said, and Miss Tims' face just lighted up with a smile.

By its glow the three of them took their departure. At the door Flora said: "Mr. Jarvis, did you get your dispatch case?" Jimmie nodded. "I found it here later, and Nick said Lem Python would see you got it."

"He did," Jimmie said. "Oh yes, indeed he did."

49

It was a great relief, Jimmie thought, to settle down to the monotony of politics. Helene was really and truly packing. Not in a huff. She had been tempted from the first offer despite its indignity. But many an artist has chiseled beauty out of an indignity, she said. Pygmalion again. Jimmie was

wistful. It gave him a charming air of melancholy. Very
good for a candidate running on a bachelor's ticket.

On Saturday night Mr. Tully was to come to dinner, all
the way to Nyack.

"Isn't it a wee bit of a strain?" Mrs. Norris asked him.

"It'd be more of a strain if I didn't," he said, and
ventured for the first time to give her a hug.

He was invited again and again and again.

ABOUT THE AUTHOR

Her crime novels have won DOROTHY SALISBURY
DAVIS a front-rank reputation, both in the United States
and abroad. For her fiction Mrs. Davis is a seven-time
Edgar Award nominee, and in 1985 she was recognized
by the Mystery Writers of America as a Grand Master
(for lifetime achievement). Among her popular and
critically acclaimed novels are A GENTLE MURDER-
ER, WHERE THE DARK STREETS GO, THE PALE
BETRAYER, A GENTLEMAN CALLED, and BLACK
SHEEP, WHITE LAMB.

DEADLY MYSTERIES

and only Robert Forsythe knows who-dunnit!

Stories by E.X. Giroux